ROCKY ROAD

ROCKY ROAD

The final part
to
Beans or Peas

DAVID P DEAN

Copyright © David P Dean, 2017

ISBN: 978-1-5486-1780-6

The right of David P Dean to be identified as the author of this work has been asserted by him in accordance with the Copyright, Designs and Patents Act 1988.

All rights reserved. No part of this publication may be reproduced, stored in a retrieval system or transmitted in any form or by any means (electronic, mechanical, photocopying, recording or otherwise), without the prior written permission of the author.

Publishing Services: The Write Factor
www.thewritefactor.co.uk

THE WRITE FACTOR

DEDICATION

This book is dedicated to Dr Vaughan Pearce and his wonderful team at the Movement Disorder Service of Exeter General Hospital (Wonford) who always gave us hope, and to the management and staff of the Palm Court Nursing Home, Dawlish, for caring.

"You never think about what life's going to be like five years down the road or ten — you just manage the day and try to make good decisions. Sometimes you do, sometimes you don't. You just hope that this day will be a good one."

-JACK HARBAUGH

★ ★ ★

"When we are no longer able to change a situation, we are challenged to change ourselves."

-VIKTOR E FRANKL

CONTENTS

Chapter 1	RAF Biggin Hill	1
Chapter 2	RAF Khormaksar, Aden	9
Chapter 3	RAF Biggin Hill	39
Chapter 4	Raf Episkopi Cyprus	47
Chapter 5	RAF Hendon	65
Chapter 6	RAF Brampton	71
Chapter 7	RAF Henlow	95
Chapter 8	Officer Cadet Training Unit	99
Chapter 9	RAF (Hospital) Ely	109
Chapter 10	RAF Brawdy	111
Chapter 11	RAF Hereford	123
Chapter 12	AFCENT	131
Chapter 13	RAF Leuchars	151
Chapter 14	RAF Kinloss	155
Chapter 15	Moving On	163
Chapter 16	The Storm	169
Chapter 17	From the Frying Pan…	177
Chapter 18	A Mixed Year	201
Chapter 19	A Heart of Pain	213
Chapter 20	The Beginning of the End	227

PREFACE

Sitting in a hospital car park wasn't part of the original plan for my day. But there I was, nevertheless – radio on, book available and the June sun streaming through the passenger side windows.

I had offered to accompany Ann into the hospital, but she assured me that it was just a woman's midlife problem which would be dealt with quickly and that I would be of no use anyway. In some ways, I was rather surprised that she wanted me along at all, particularly as she had her own car and that the problem, in her words, was "trifling". But, she'd asked me to go and that was enough to persuade me to travel to the hospital with her. I realised she just needed a bit of moral support. The only thing that she'd ever asked of me which was of great importance, and it was more of a statement than a request was that – "You can't leave me now!"

★ ★ ★

The year was 1986. It was just over two decades before that Ann and I had returned from Singapore – our first overseas tour. Two decades of monumental change had followed, not only in my career, but also, and probably more so, in ourselves. In many ways, it had been twenty years of turmoil.

To reach this point in time, the Corporal Dixie Dean of 1965 had needed to undergo a metamorphosis. All of this change had come about though with the loving support and encouragement of Ann, my wife. Without her beside me, there is no doubt whatsoever that the author of this book would still be Corporal Dixie Dean and not Squadron Leader Dixie Dean. She asked so little of me during that time and yet gave so much. Hence, it wasn't difficult to agree to accompany her to the hospital, but I suspected the visit was slightly more important than she had led me to believe.

I arrived at RAF Kinloss in September 1985, having been promoted to Squadron Leader, the Officer Commanding the Catering Squadron. It is still a constant wonder to me how I managed to progress through the ranks – seven in all – in order to attain my current position. For my part, there was the love of my trade – cooking and all the other aspects of catering. But the truth is, that alone is insufficient to attain high rank in the Royal Air Force, particularly if you come from the rank and file, like I did. No, you also need your own guru or gurus – a lodestar almost – and a good woman. And I had both. Between them, they honed the old Dixie Dean, rubbing off most of his rough edges and allowing him to brush up the finished product – even though I still remain somewhat roughly polished! Somehow, despite all this, I never seemed to lose the arrogance of the younger Dean or the need to challenge authority. But now though, I knew where the line was drawn.

To put the Dixie Dean of 1986 into perspective, we need to return to the past – just to see how life remodelled him.

CHAPTER 1

RAF BIGGIN HILL

It was 1965 and my next tour of duty after leaving Singapore was to be RAF Biggin Hill. As a family, we quickly settled into married quarters at the station and I started work as the NCO in charge of a shift in the Airmen's Mess. In every serviceman's life, there will be two or three events which make each tour memorable. They may be, of course, memorable in a good way or in a bad way, but something always rises up out of the humdrum, day-in, day-out episodes of life that makes you return to that period in your mind ever after and think, "Yes! That was important". They are probably thought of now as 'defining moments'. And so it was with Biggin Hill. The job wasn't particularly interesting, but I enjoyed it. It wasn't difficult work, so with a little effort, it was easy to shine – and I made that little extra effort. On top of that, I joined the committee of the Junior Rank's Club and helped organise social events. I enjoyed it and it turned out I had something to offer. The following year, July 1966, together with a friend of mine, John – who held a brown belt in judo, as opposed to my lower green – we opened a judo club on the station, for all-comers. With the consent of the Station Commander, it was also opened to the local civilian population.

After several weeks of advertising and an awful lot of hard work spent arranging accommodation and equipment, that first evening we enrolled 205 members, ranging from three year olds to 63 year olds. Everybody, it seemed, had watched the latest James Bond film, *Goldfinger*, and wanted to learn to fight. It was a hugely rewarding period for me, not least because one of the younger children was my eldest son, Tony. Nevertheless, it was an incredibly busy and difficult time, due to having to sift through the huge number of applicants – there were, after all, only two of us at the helm. It was absolute mayhem! We had suggested in the advertising that, on the first night, we would gather at 18.00 hrs in order to take names, sort people into age and ability groups, give a little welcome speech, highlighting our aims – and then we thought we might even get a little judo in. That was not the case! By 22.00 hrs, we had sorted out all the adults with very young children so they could get them home, and had taken the names of all those who had turned up. As a result, my little welcome speech was aimed specifically at the parents with very young children. Because of the large number of those who wanted to take part, the lowest age for training had to be set at five years. Although that disappointed some, the parents were wise enough to realise that we just wouldn't be able to manage, even with their offers of help. Unfortunately, that only reduced the total numbers by seven.

Over the next three weeks, with help from a couple of the attendees who had some judo experience and, eventually, one PTI (Physical Training Instructor) on loan from the station gymnasium, we sorted the 198 attendees into three main groups: five to eight year olds, nine to 15 year olds and adults – i.e. anyone over 16 years old, which comprised the largest group of about 125. We decided that, during the first month, we would do some serious sifting. The five to eight year olds, of which there were about 30, were to attend twice a week – Mondays and Thursdays, from 18.00 to 19.00 hrs. The 9 to 15 year olds, which totalled about 40 individuals, attended from 19.30 to 20.30. 40 people was about the maximum number to fit comfortably into the Nissen hut, which was our allocated accommodation, without bumping into one another. The remaining 125 were split into three groups, and by general agreement, they were to attend once a week on a Tuesday, Wednesday or Friday for two hours from 19.00 to 21.00.

Very few had judokas, the suit you fight in, but our plan for the first four weeks didn't require them. We had made it very clear from the outset that judo was a very physical sport and that you, therefore, had to be both very fit and committed. So, with a lot of help from our PTI and together with my own knowledge and John's experience, we set out a rigorous month's fitness training, starting always with a short run of about two to three miles, followed by training in the 'Club Room', covering everything that I remembered from my own training in the Budaqoix, together with John's and the PTI, Pete's experience. We were a little kinder with the five to eight year olds, knowing that any kind of physical training would put many off.

The outcome was, as anticipated, that by the middle of August 1966, we had thinned out the total number of members to 104! This meant that we could now run the course in two groups. The only five year old left was Tony, my eldest son, and the next child was seven. Hence we combined the two age groups together, giving us one class of 36 children, ranging from Tony at five to 15 year olds – and they continued to attend a class twice a week from 18.30 to 19.30. The remaining participants, now a more manageable number of 68, were divided into two classes of 34 each and they also attended twice a week, with one group following the youngsters, which was a Monday and Thursday, starting at 20.00 until we finished (this could be anytime between 21.30 and 22.00) and the other groups on Wednesdays and Fridays ran at similar times.

This was still a huge commitment, but, with the continuing help of Pete (the PTI) in the children's classes, plus myself, John, and the two airmen who had some judo experience, we also successfully ran the adult classes. We swapped teachers many times over the following year as the syllabus we followed was, by and large, the same. The adults were to be graded as yellow belts and the younger children were to have a red flash on their white belts. The gradings all took place in London and, within the first year, 43 adults had gained their yellow belt – one of whom remains a dear friend to this day – and many became helpers in our now growing club. We lost about 12 students for various reasons. Of the children, however, 22 gained their red flash and we lost about 9 or 10, again for different causes. In the main, though, the numbers remained stable. For those we lost, there were always some who wanted to join.

Alas, for me, my time at Biggin Hill had run its course. I was promoted to Sergeant and posted to the Middle East in July 1967 on a nine-month unaccompanied tour. Ann and the boys moved, by choice, to RAF Denbury, which now accommodated families whilst husbands were on tour. The choice, incidentally, didn't include staying at Biggin Hill which, of course, would have been her first preference. Like most things though, she just took the disruption in her stride. We didn't own a great deal of furniture, but what we did have, plus all our small items, Ann packed into boxes which were removed by a company, courtesy of the RAF. The removal van arrived on Monday afternoon and, other than a few overnight items, everything we owned had been loaded onto the van. The arrangements were that we would travel by train and arrive at Denbury by 14.00 hrs on the Tuesday to take over a married quarter where Ann and the boys would live whilst I was abroad.

I reported to the guardroom at RAF Denbury just after lunch on the Tuesday – the journey had taken about four hours – and then I signed for the keys to the house. Seeing that we were on foot and looking somewhat bedraggled, the Sergeant in the guardroom arranged for someone to drive us down to the village where the married quarters were situated. Of course, Denbury was well known to both of us. I had been posted there in late 1958 and Ann shortly after. Less than a year later, in the August of 1959, we had got married and because we were too young to qualify for married quarters, we'd lived happily in a caravan for the next two and a half years until we left for Singapore. In the March of 1962, when we left for Singapore, we only had one son, Tony, who was fourteen months old, but five and half years later, we had three sons: Tony, the eldest, Colin, nearly two years younger, and Andrew, who had been born on 30th June 1965. Both Colin and Andrew had been born in Singapore.

I had mixed feelings about our return to Denbury, although I could understand why Ann chose it. It was familiar and having been there for so long before, there were bound to be faces that Ann remembered. But, for me, there were lots of mixed memories. The tyrannical Sergeant Magin who had made my early years an absolute misery; Warrant Officer Pocock, the Station Warrant Officer, who was cut from the same cloth – and so many others, not to mention my long stint in detention – trouble seemed to follow me wherever I went back then. And then Ann had arrived, my beloved Ann, and suddenly my troubles were diluted. Through her, I saw life from a different perspective. And here we were, back at Denbury, me now a Sergeant with all that entitles you to – not least married quarters!

CHAPTER 2

RAF KHORMAKSAR, ADEN

The removal van arrived on time and, by 18.00 hrs, we were settled in, bags unpacked, sticks of furniture in the right places, beds made and some of the neighbours had even popped in to say hello – mostly wives whose husbands were abroad. That was a sharp reminder that, on the coming Friday, I would be leaving again – this time for nine months.

Even after all these years, I can still see the faces of Ann and the children when I left that morning. This family isn't into the 'stiff upper lip', although Ann tried for the sake of the children. However, it soon became clear to them that something important was happening. Andrew, who was, after all, only just two years old, seeing the trembling lip of his mother and the tears of his six year old brother, soon broke down and cried too – although I'm sure he didn't really know what was going on. Their little faces have stayed with me, and I can see them even as I write this. But, as I have said many times, it is the way of service life that we are always saying goodbye.

I was being posted to Bahrain in the Persian Gulf, but once on board the aircraft, we were informed by a Flight Lieutenant that a number of personnel were being posted to RAF Khormaksar in Aden. Therefore, that would be our first port of call. Those personnel bound for units further afield were to stay on board. I have to say, I thought that was rather strange. Having travelled this way before – whilst on the way to Singapore – I knew that the flight path would take us to Bahrain first. Nevertheless, it all became clear – well, clearer, anyway. As we approached the airspace over Yemen at the bottom end of Saudi Arabia, we were told to buckle up as the landing at RAF Khormaksar might be bumpy. They were right – not only was it bumpy because large areas of the runway had been blown up, but it was also frighteningly noisy with explosions occurring all around us. The aircraft weaved left and right, lost height and then seemed to fight to gain height again. Amidst all this mayhem, the aircraft eventually found a path that took us down to RAF Khormaksar, albeit with spine-shaking results. With the brakes screaming, the aircraft crisscrossed the runway, throwing us wildly left and right, our bodies straining against the seat belts. Having avoided most of the larger bomb craters, the aircraft lurched to a halt near some hangars. It took just minutes to get all the personnel off and into safety within RAF Khormaksar. In this organised chaos, we literally ran, exiting the aircraft to this so-called safety zone. All the while, the noise of shell fire was continuous amidst the screams of those in charge to, "Keep running!" I needed no encouragement. When I had the opportunity to look back, the aircraft was already moving with a view, I guessed, to take off – it was pretty much a sitting target where it was.

Once inside the hangar-type building, all we could hear was small arms fire with, what we found out later was a grenade attack. This continued for a little while and then, suddenly, it all went quiet. We found out subsequently that another aircraft, a Douglas DC3, had been bombed in mid-air earlier in the year, killing all the people on board. It seemed that our saviours that day were the 1st Argyll and Sutherland Highlanders led by a Lt. Col. Colin Mitchell, who was respectfully known by his command as 'Mad Mitch'. They had arrived in Aden about ten days earlier, having taken over from 45 Commando, a regiment close to my heart.

The conflict in Aden goes back many years. The 'Emergency' as we know it, only really flared in 1963 though. The perceived anti-colonial uprising that year provided an opportunity for the Egyptian leader, Gamel Abdel Nasser, to continue his threat under the guise of the NFL: the Egyptian-backed National Liberation Front, alongside the tribes of the Radfan area of the country who formed the Front for the Liberation of Occupied South Yemen (FLOSY). Although they often fought each other, as well as the British, their joint aim was to get the British out of South Yemen. That message was rammed home when, on the 10th December of that year, the NFL attacked the British High Commissioner as he arrived at RAF Khormaksar to board an aircraft for London. One woman was killed and 50 others injured. A State of Emergency was declared that day.

Although thereafter much of the violence was carried out in the Crater, the old Arab quarter of Aden, the fighting had spread. Most of the guerrilla attacks were focused on off-duty British personnel and policemen, but not exclusively. An attack against RAF Khormaksar resulted in the death and injury of many children at a party. The Emergency was exacerbated by the Six Day War in June 1967. Nasser claimed that the British had helped Israel in this war and this led to a mutiny by hundreds of soldiers in the South Arabian Army who, on the 20th June, killed 22 British soldiers and shot down a helicopter. As a direct result, the Crater was occupied by rebel forces. It was at that point that all British families were evacuated. That mutiny resulted in continuing guerrilla warfare with gun battles, arson, looting and frequent murders. Order was finally restored that July with the arrival of the Argyll and Sutherland Highlanders. Nevertheless, deadly attacks by the NFL and FLOSY continued against the British forces, resulting in our withdrawal from Aden on 30th November, 1967.

As I sat on my kit bag after that eventful flight, I have to say I was pretty shaken, but most of what I have just recorded was at that point still unknown to me. All I really knew was there were clearly problems in Aden and I, thankfully, was continuing north to Bahrain.

We sat around for most of the morning with strict instructions not to venture out, although most of the gunfire I could hear seemed to come from some distance away. The longer we sat there, the warmer it became though. There didn't seem to be any windows and the ceiling fans, which seemed to be working at full speed, hardly moved the air. After several hours, we were finally called to order by the same Flight Lieutenant who was on board. He jumped up on a table so he could be seen and heard easily. He quickly explained the immediate problem and that things were now under control. With that, he shouted above the noise of the fans that the following personnel were to gather together by an entrance which he indicated.

I have to say that I wasn't surprised when I heard my name called as I suspected that all of us there were en route to Bahrain, so it made sense to separate us out from those being retained at Khormaksar. There were about 12 of us called and I knew none of the other men. All of us were looking pretty pleased with ourselves and there was a bit of elbow nudging and a little laughter, plus a few comments along the lines of, "I won't be sorry to see the back of this place," and "You can't help but feel sorry for the poor buggers left behind" and so on. The

Flight Lieutenant made his way through the remaining crowd which numbered about 80 to 100 and addressed the 12 of us.

"I believe that you were expecting to carry on your journey to Bahrain in the very near future? Unfortunately, your onward journey has been delayed!" Deadly silence. He continued, "I don't know for how long – that will depend upon your respective squadrons. But, for now, you are to report to your various headquarters who will assign you your accommodation and duties."

Everybody had a question and all at the same time. He raised a hand to shut us up. "There is no point in asking me any questions," he said, "because I have no answers – I am also being retained. Report to your various squadron headquarters. They, I'm sure, will have the answers to your questions."

It turned out that the Flight Lieutenant was a catering officer named Rose, who would have been my boss in Bahrain as the deputy to the Squadron Commander. Instead, he would join three other junior officers under the command of a Squadron Leader, who for the purpose of this narrative, we will call Fenton and who I'd been led to believe was a tyrant! His was a name familiar to all caterers. 'Tyrant,' I believe, is the wrong noun for him though. He was exacting in his standards and mostly they were applied to his officers but, unfortunately, his leadership style filtered down to his senior NCOs. He was quite an incredible man – with many marathons under his belt. He also competed in the 'Iron Man' event which is exceptionally gruelling – and he won! He was a hard-drinking, rough, tough individual who was always up for a challenge.

My arrival interview went badly though. In response to my question, "How long am I likely to be at Khormaksar?" his reply was, "You will be here for as long as necessary, Sergeant Dean, and like me, you won't be leaving until the job's done!" Other than that, it was a straightforward arrival interview – until we got to the part when he asked me what I did in my spare time. I mentioned that I enjoyed judo and that I hoped that there was a club at Khormaksar.

"Ah, so you like to fight, do you, Sergeant Dean?"

I wasn't sure of my answer, so I simply said, "Yes, within the confines of a judo club."

He went on to say that he knew nothing about judo, but he doubted that if he got me in some sort of self-defence hold that I would be able to break free. Not quite sure what I was getting myself into, I simply said, "I don't think that would be the case, but I hope I will never be put to the test."

With that, he just smiled and said, "Report to the Combined Mess," which was catering for Warrant Officers, SNCOs and airmen. "My office will instruct you on your accommodation and other duties. Dismissed!"

I left his office with a feeling of foreboding – I was certain that one day I would have to pay for my remarks.

One of the airmen from his office escorted me to a married quarter on the edge of the unit which was to be my accommodation, shared with four other NCOs. As we neared the outer edge of the unit, the airman said, "Be careful from now on, Sarge, there's been quite a bit of sniper fire from those buildings over there". He was pointing to a selection of buildings outside the wire and about 150 yards from my accommodation. "Mostly it's around the middle of the day, but you can never be sure, so hug the buildings until you're inside. It never lasts long and the Argyll's soon see them off." He said this in such a matter of fact manner that it took a little while for it to register. But, when it did, I thought, "Is he joking – some bastard is actually going to shoot at me, just because I'm going to work? Why don't they just move us further into the safety of the unit?" Mine was not to reason why though! What seemed worse than that, at the time, was that the only bed available was a double – like I wasn't missing Ann enough!

There is a danger that this episode of my tale might become a little domesticated. So, because this is a warzone, I will try and extract the salient points of the war and how they affected me, and leave out most of the day-to-day domestic crap. It was now 23rd July.

The Combined Mess was feeding about 1600 personnel at each main meal. Besides the three main meals, there were also duty suppers – the first at 22.00 hrs going on until midnight and again at about 02.30 until early breakfast which started at 05.30. All these additional meals were to accommodate the enormous number of people on guard duty. In short, we were producing food

24 hours a day. The first duty supper until breakfast could also include officers, of which there were about 200. At that time, we could be feeding up to 2000 personnel over the course of 24 hours. That number increased through August and September to about 3000 and then started to reduce as the wheels of withdrawal started to grind. The withdrawal date, we were informed, was 30th November, 1967. There were no days off as such, but the shifts were set up so you only worked eight hours in every 24 on a fixed cyclical system. Day One: 14.00 to 22.00. Day Two: 06.00 to 14.00. Day Three: 22.00 to 06.00. Hence although we didn't get much time off between the late and early shifts, we did get 32 hours off between the early shift and the following night shift which compensated for this. Not that there was anything to do. We weren't allowed off the unit, so we just slept or sunbathed.

The only distractions or additions to these shifts was your guard duty which was 24 hours every 7 days and this could be internal (installations, buildings and so on) or external (the perimeter wire) and these shifts could really bugger up your time off. The shift on guard was two hours on and four hours off through the 24 hours and then you were expected to pick up your next available shift in the mess. Not that missing a shift made much difference. Like Singapore, where I'd been between 1962 and1965, most of the work was done by the local staff. In this case, Arabs or Egyptians. In the Combined Mess, these local staff totalled about 25. So with almost the equivalent number of UK personnel on each shift, there were about 16 to 20 workers. And that was just in the kitchen. The dining room, plate washing team and so on had their own complement of workers, also mostly local.

The kitchen was run by a Flight Sergeant, called Stoke, who, strangely enough, had been a Sergeant Instructor at the School of Catering when I went through in 1956/57 – but he didn't remember me. The dining room was run by a Sergeant Steward whose name I can never remember. The whole mess was overseen by a Warrant Officer called Behan who I saw about ten times during the five months I was there and most of those times it was in the Catering Club – a sort of private club that someone had set up years before for all ranks, so long as you were a caterer, of course. There were still the usual clubs attributed to your rank – a Corporals' Club, for drinks only, and a Sergeants' Mess, but that only served alcohol, as they joined the lower ranks in the Combined Mess for dining. Of course, there was also an Officers' Mess that provided all services up until the closing of the bar. But, and it's a big but – Squadron Leader Fenton liked all caterers, regardless of rank, to use the Catering Club. This, I found out, was not a request. You were considered disloyal if you didn't use it and there would be consequences! This, of course, meant that on or off duty, unless you were elsewhere of course, you were always under scrutiny.

He used the club as a Colonel of a regiment might use a Regimental Mess! He was recognised as the head of the mess and was feted accordingly! In some ways, I didn't actually mind using the club – or I didn't mind the idea of it. As a newly promoted Sergeant, the Sergeants' Mess was still something I had to get used to. I still felt like an outsider. At least in the Catering Club, I felt I belonged.

Having said that – remember those defining moments in each tour? – I'd been there about a fortnight and I had what I thought was an acceptable routine which hadn't thus far included many visits to the Catering Club. Primarily, this was because whatever free time I had, if I wasn't sleeping, I was at the judo club. It turned out that it was a very active club, not least, because the Argylls were now there, but it had, over and above them, about 40 other members anyway. Because of our crazy shift patterns, you could almost always find someone there from about 10.00 hrs onwards. It was well organised with one home-grown black belt, two brown belts and an assortment of others. But, and again it's a big but, with the arrival of the Argylls in their numbers, they had three black belts and one was a 3rd Dan! Plus, they had in their number about 10 or 12 other assorted belts, so I was in my element and really had no reason to socialise elsewhere because they also had a bar!

On this one particular day, it was about 16.00 hrs and I was on the late shift. We were just about to fill the servery with food for early teas when suddenly I was grabbed from behind and held in a vice-like grip – a sort of half-nelson with my left arm pinned behind me. The pressure on my neck from my assailant's wrist was quite painful. Thinking it was one of the lads messing about because they all knew I enjoyed judo, I just said, "Okay, I give in – you win."

"I'm afraid it isn't that easy, Sergeant Dean." The voice was Fenton's. "If you want to carry on working, you will have to break my hold."

"Are you joking, sir?" I said. "We're in the middle of a kitchen – someone will get hurt!"

"Ah," he said, strengthening his hold, "are you saying you can't break the hold?"

"No," I said, now in quite a lot of pain. "I'm just saying that someone will get hurt."

"Well, it won't be me, Sergeant Dean," he replied, "so, either break the hold or give in and concede that I'm the better man."

"Would it help, sir, if I told you that I can break the hold, but you will get hurt?"

I know all this sounds ridiculous, but I guess you need to know what manner of man he was. Meanwhile, all work in the kitchen had ceased and no one was filling the servery with food. In fact, they were just standing around, awaiting the outcome.

I repeated, "I can get out of the hold, sir, but you will get hurt!"

"I promise," he said, "that you will not be held responsible for the outcome – everybody here is my witness!"

I resigned myself to the fact that he was not going to release me. So, regardless of the outcome, I decided that I would release myself. Assessing his body contact, I quickly put my left foot and upper body forward which opened up just enough space between his front and my back to displace his balance. In the same instant, I hooked my right bent leg backwards with the intention of heeling him in the bollocks. It didn't make full contact, but it hurt enough for him to loosen his grip and for me to grab his right shirt front with my left hand and pull him across my right hip, aided now by my right leg, which I swept back to finish the job. But for my kindness, he would have landed badly, so I assisted his fall. Was he grateful? Was he shit!

"You cheated!" he shouted. "A kick in the nuts is not judo!"

"You're right, sir", I said, "but I did say I could get out of your hold – and I did – and I did miss your nuts, sir!"

He stormed out shouting, "I expect to see you in the club tomorrow night, Sergeant Dean – that's an order!"

When he was what everybody thought to be a safe distance away, they all broke into rapturous applause. Somewhat over-confident, I smiled and bowed from the waist at my audience, but I was thinking, "I haven't heard the last of that – Fenton will not forget."

The following night I turned up at the Catering Club, as ordered. It was quite busy and, although I saw the Squadron Leader out of the corner of my eye at the bar, talking to a couple of Warrant Officers, one of whom I recognised as the Officers' Mess manager, I made my way to a small group of people mostly from the Combined Mess. Amongst them was Flight Sergeant Stoke, my immediate boss in the kitchen. They all smiled and we exchanged greetings. Someone asked me if I would like a drink, but I declined – simply because I wasn't thirsty.

Flight Sergeant Stoke lowered his voice, checking to make sure that Fenton was still at the bar. "You know he's going to get back at you tonight, don't you?"

"And here's me thinking that he invited me along to buy me a drink and let bygones be bygones," I replied.

Stoke smiled. "Well, in some ways that's exactly what he's going to do." He went on to say, "Have you ever drunk a yard of ale?"

"A yard of ale?" I replied. "I've never even heard of a yard of ale, let alone drunk one!"

"Without making it obvious," he said, "just above Fenton, on the wall behind the bar, you'll see a huge glass that looks like a trumpet at one end with a large orb of glass at the other – well, that's a yard."

"Bloody hell," I said. "How much beer does that hold?"

He went on to explain that that particular yard held about two and three quarter pints and that I would have to drink it all without spilling any.

"I don't really have to, do I?"

He looked at me out of the corner of his eye. "If you don't," he said, "he'll make your life a bloody misery – and you're not exactly his favourite person, are you? Look, meet me outside in about two minutes and I'll give you some quick instructions on how to drink from a yard!"

RAF KHORMAKSAR, ADEN

I excused myself a couple of minutes later and met the Flight Sergeant behind the building. He went on to explain that you held the yard with both hands and then, when it was full, the moment your lips touch liquid, you should slowly spin the glass in your hands. "Keep spinning and you can drink as slowly as you like, but don't take your lips off the glass and don't stop spinning because, if you do, the liquid will wash up from the orb and you will be covered in beer! An' that's what he's hoping for – so don't give him the pleasure!"

I thanked him and quickly nipped into the loo just in case somebody came looking for me. And, sure enough, just as I was leaving, I bumped into the Warrant Officers' Mess manager. "Oh, Sergeant Dean," he said. "The Squadron Leader was looking for you. He thought perhaps you'd gone back to your bunk?"

"As if I would, sir, and deprive the Squadron Leader the opportunity of buying me a drink!"

Although he only smiled in response, I felt sure that he was on my side – the smile had a sort of sympathetic edge to it. No sooner had I walked into the bar with the Warrant Officer following, than a shout went up from the other side of the room.

"Attention everybody!" Having gained the attention of everybody in the room, the Squadron Leader now addressed the assembled crowd. "In the time-honoured tradition, we would like to welcome Sergeant Dean to our number!" he continued, with what I thought was a malicious glint in his eye. "So far, he hasn't attended 'our' Club as often as we would like, having made friends in other quarters. However, we are the forgiving kind" – a gentle titter rose from the assembled crowd – "so, tonight, we shall formally initiate him into our little group and, hopefully, that will encourage him to attend on a more regular basis!"

He went on to explain that all I had to do to become an 'accepted' member was to stand inside the circle. He now indicated a circle which was about 24" in diameter and, as predicted, he said I must drink a yard of ale – the choice of ale could be mine. As someone was retrieving the yard from behind the bar, I asked, "Does it have to be ale?"

He just smirked. "It's called a yard of ale, Sergeant Dean. You wouldn't want to fill it with lemonade, would you?"

With that everybody laughed and joined in the joke. Everybody except, I noticed, Flight Lieutenant Rose, the officer who had briefed us on our arrival. I couldn't read his face, but it seemed to hold sympathy, so I had a few allies out there!

In answer to the type of beer I wanted, I simply said that I didn't really drink beer, so the weakest they had would be fine.

The Squadron Leader shouted out, "Barman, fill the yard with your weakest ale for Sergeant Dean!"

I wasn't given any instructions, other than I had to remain in the circle. Once my lips touched the beer, I couldn't remove them until the yard was empty.

"Of course, if you fail Sergeant Dean," said a now gloating Fenton, "you will have to repeat the ceremony at a later date!"

After my earlier instructions on how to drink a yard, I was feeling reasonably confident. The yard arrived, filled absolutely to the brim. I thought I detected a look of warning or sympathy from the barman. I wasn't sure. He then just turned and left me holding the yard – which was already spilling a little.

"Right, Sergeant Dean, on the count of three – are you ready?"

I nodded and to the cries of "Down! Down!" I placed the yard on my lips and, as instructed, I started to spin it very slowly. Although it all seemed incredibly slow, it worked. The ale slowly revolved around inside the yard and, as long as the liquid touched my lips, I was consuming it within the rules – so I didn't care if it took all night. But, I could only have drunk about a third of the ale when I started to feel incredibly dizzy. I stopped swallowing, and kept spinning the yard, but it was no use – I just knew I was going to faint. As I started to fall, I stopped spinning the yard, so the best part of two pints of ale washed all over me and, at the same time, almost as though he knew, Flight Sergeant Stoke relieved me of the now empty yard and I collapsed, soaked, onto the floor.

The next thing I remember is a couple of people helping me to a chair. Flight Sergeant Stoke came over to see if I was okay. "What the hell happened?" I said. "I seemed to be doing alright and suddenly I felt faint – it was almost as though the beer had gone straight to my head! It was only light ale, wasn't it?" I asked.

"Yes," he said, hesitating. "I think so – well, that's what I asked for!" He gave me a knowing smile. "Between you and me, I think there might have been a little extra in the drink!"

With that, the Squadron Leader approached. "Poor show, Sergeant Dean, better luck next time!" With that, he came a little closer to me so only I could hear and said, "He who laughs last …" And, with that, he walked away.

I would like to be able to say that life settled into dull routine after that – but life at Khormaksar was never dull. By the middle of August, there had been several incidents – a few of them personal. After one such incident, I was moved from the Combined Mess to the so-called 'Khormaksar Hotel'. This mess had really grown out of the closure of the 'Red Sea Hotel', which was in the Crater area of Aden – and, although British troops had re-entered the Crater with force, it was clearly an unsafe place for visitors to be – hence the Khormaksar Hotel came about. I will explain what I mean by 'visitors' later, but for now, here's an explanation as to why I was moved.

I had probably been in Aden for about a month and I had worked, as I have said, in the Combined Mess as an NCO I/C and I'd been on shift for most of that time. It wasn't work that I enjoyed – I seemed to spend most of my time pushing people along to meet the deadline of the mealtimes, which as I have said, were four times in every 24 hours. The workforce was made up of Arabs, Egyptians and, of course, Brits. By August, there seemed to be, at times, a reluctance on the part of the local staff to apply the same urgency to meet these deadlines. With hindsight, one can only assume that there were those amongst their number who did not have our best interests at heart and this was one way of creating disruption. I am not saying it was all of them – but there were certainly one or two on each shift who could influence the rest. Such was the case on this particular day. I have no idea how or what started it, but 15 minutes before the main servery was set up, with a queue already reaching about four hundred, a row broke out between a local cook and a local kitchen hand. Before we realised it, there were two factions, Arab and Egyptian, in an incredibly noisy, violent stand-off. Myself and three others tried to intervene, but within a blink of an eye, both sides sat down on the floor, refusing to work. Everything came to a standstill. The Flight Sergeant had now joined us, wondering what all the noise was about. Seeing the situation, he instructed the Brits to pick up the trays of food which had been on the way to the servery when the incident occurred, but which were now on the floor beside the seated locals. Any attempt by the British staff to remove the trays was violently fought off by the seated locals, and this was all orchestrated by, it seemed to me, a local Arab kitchen hand who we, or I, had had problems with before.

Now, I don't know if it was tiredness or I was pissed off because it was my shift that was being disrupted, or just an accumulation of events, but I bent down and grabbed hold of the wrist of the Arab kitchen hand, who I believed to be the ringleader, and dragged his skinny arse across the kitchen and preparation room. He was kicking and screaming all the way and I dumped him in the back yard, locking the door behind me.

Interestingly enough, no one came to his aid. With him still screaming and shouting, I returned to find that the rest of the locals, encouraged by Flight Sergeant Stoke, had risen from the floor and were now loading trays of food into the servery. As far as I was concerned, that should have been an end to it. Alas, life isn't that simple. Through some sort of civilian administrative intervention, I was charged with assault – apparently, he'd got a bruised wrist – brought about, reluctantly, by Flight Sergeant Stoke. I was remanded to the Station Commander.

So, not for the first time, I found myself facing the Station Commander on a charge of assault. The last time, I had been at RAF Denbury and I'd struck an airman because he couldn't decide whether he wanted beans or peas. That assault, I've come to believe, was without mitigation, so I accepted and deserved the detention imposed upon me and I had no one to speak up for me. Not so this time. Although he was obliged to charge me, Flight Sergeant Stoke, plus three other Brits spoke on my behalf. More importantly, an Egyptian chef also offered to speak up for me. Apparently, I had nipped in the bud what could have become an inflammatory racial incident. Nevertheless, I was reprimanded and it was noted on my file and I was moved from the Combined Mess to the Khormaksar Hotel.

Incidentally, that same Arab was shot about six weeks later by the British Forces. Apparently, he had shot and killed an off-duty airman, a Sergeant, at a petrol station just outside the Khormaksar main gate – what the hell he was doing there, one can only guess – and they also attributed three other deaths to my 'bruised wristed' Arab.

Several things happened during the following week that slightly altered my brain-dead routine. Firstly, there were no shifts as such at the 'hotel'. Admittedly, it was a 14-hour working day, providing the three main meals, but any meals outside these hours were, as in the Officers' Mess, taken in the Combined Mess. For my part, I worked the 'tropical day', which was 07.00 until 13.00 hrs, but I was always around for the main meal, which again, like the Officers' Mess, was in the evening.

The other important change for me was that the 'powers that be' had decided to vacate all the accommodation on the outer fringes of the unit – and not before time, in my opinion. Running the daily gauntlet just to get to work was becoming tiresome. For my part, I now had my own room in the hotel. But by far the most heart-lifting part was that Ian (Spike) Daw, who had been my friend for years – I was even the best man at his wedding – had arrived at Khormaksar for the withdrawal.

Jane, his wife, had also opted to be housed at Denbury for the duration. So, not only did Ann have company, but so did I. Life, just suddenly, felt so much better. And in various ways, it continued like that for a while.

The hotel catered for all visitors, regardless of rank, or whether they were in the service or civilians – although they dined at separate tables. Most of the civilians were drawn from stage and screen work to entertain the troops under the CSE (Combined Services Entertainment) umbrella, and for whatever reason, this programme attracted a lot of big name entertainers. If I was really cynical, I might say that this scheme also propped up a lot of flagging careers. But, during the time I was working in the Khormaksar Hotel, we catered for Mike and Bernie Winters – Bernie we'll talk more of later – Sandie Shaw, a bare-footed pop singer, Bob Monkhouse, Tony Hancock and so many more. All of these 'named' celebrities travelled with dozens of other lesser known entertainers, so that each show was made up of three acts – a singer, a comedian and a variety act, i.e. a ventriloquist, conjuror and so on, with the named entertainer topping the bill. They also travelled with a large number of other people, all of whom were needed to make the show work. Starlets? Well, you have to have dancers, don't you? Roadies, dressers, make-up people, a director and many more – they all had a role to play. During the time I was in Aden, there must have been eight or nine of these shows of which the cast of six stayed in the Khormaksar Hotel.

In order to avoid the fine line between anecdote and libel, I will just say that the after-show activities were often just as entertaining as the shows! In getting up close to some of these people, I soon realised how fragile their world was – and how frequently they have to resort to additional aid in order to perform. Whether that be drink, drugs, sex or just someone to massage their egos! However, on a lighter note, one of the nicest people I have ever met was Bernie Winters. What you saw on stage and TV was really what you got with him. He was a happy, gregarious, fun-loving individual who was completely at ease in his own skin – and he had no airs and graces. One night, after the show, I believe it was the last night, but I can't really remember, the PMC (President of the Messing Committee) and officers invited the cast back to the Officers' Mess for drinks. As had been the case on several occasions, some of us watched the shows from the wings, simply because we had got to know some of the 'celebrities' well and they had invited us. Such was the case when Mike and Bernie Winters performed. Bernie asked Spike and me if we would like to join him for a drink after the show, and of course, we agreed – not realising at the time that the after-show entertainment was to be held in the Officers' Mess! By the time we did realise this, we were closing in on the mess, fast.

I said to Bernie, "We can't go in there, it's for officers only!" I was really beginning to panic.

"Oh, that's alright," Bernie said, "I'll tell them you're friends of mine!" And, with that, he's pushing us up the stairs where the PMC and his committee are waiting to greet their guests.

"Congratulations, Mr. Winters, on a first class show!"

"Thank you," he replied. "Please call me Bernie. I'd like to introduce you to a couple of friends of mine, this is …"

"Spring!" I said, a little too loudly.

Bernie and Spike both looked at me, not sure what to say. "Flying Officer David Spring, sir," I blurted out. "Newly arrived Catering Officer."

A hand reached for mine and shook it. "Welcome to the Mess, David." I looked up and almost filled my trousers – it was Lt. Col. Mitchell of the Argyll and Sutherland Highlanders! I was shaking hands with Mad Mitch! Whilst this was going on, Spike, realising the problem, jumped the queue with Bernie's help and disappeared into the crowd.

When we met up about two minutes later, drinks in hand, Spike said, "Spring? Where the fucking hell did 'Spring' come from!"

I looked at Bernie and smiled. "It was his fault," I said, pointing at Bernie. "When he said 'Winters', Spring was all I could think of!"

We didn't stay long, making our excuses to Bernie and pointing out that we could yet meet our boss, Sqn. Ldr. Fenton. We slipped out a side door and laughed all the way back to the hotel.

Just as an aside, about a month later, Col. Mitchell, with other colleagues, was inspecting the hotel with a view to determining what should be destroyed before handover to the Saudi Arabian authorities on the 30th November. As common courtesy, I was introduced to the Colonel because I was running the kitchen. I tried not to look up as he shook my hand, but that was impossible, of course.

"We've met before, haven't we?" he asked.

"No, I don't believe so, sir – although I do know you by sight, sir." He just hung onto my hand a little too long.

"Mmm!" he muttered, "I never forget a face. Never mind," he said, as he released my hand, "it'll come back to me!"

To my knowledge, it never did.

I had three withdrawal dates for my departure – W-17 which was cancelled after closing down the hotel, and W-9 which, along with many others after closing down the Officers' Mess, was also cancelled. I finally got away on W-4. But I'm getting a bit ahead of myself. Spike continued to work in the Combined Mess and, like me, didn't get away until nearly the end. The last four to six weeks were pretty bad. The firing and shelling had got a lot closer, but fortunately, it was always held in check, not least by the Argylls. Within the confines of Khormaksar, which had shrunk considerably as the perimeter fence had been drawn in making it easier to defend, us service personnel had now become more and more aware of the civilians who were left. The Egyptians were still hoping that the British would take them home – for being left behind meant certain death. The Arabs, as a result of one or two killings inside the unit, were all now being viewed with suspicion. We were all living on edge, not really knowing who to trust or when we were likely to actually leave. Of course, most of the time we were too busy or too tired to think. Spike suffered quite a bit though and, unfortunately, left the service soon after returning home.

All accommodation was now centred in an area called The Twinnings and all feeding was from the Combined Mess. From these areas came a corridor, of sorts, which led down to the runway. And that was to be our route out when our time came.

There's something I have forgotten, but is worth a mention. All of the rations we now had comprised the entirety of what we were going to get. Let me explain. Up until recently, and we are now within four weeks of W-Day, we were collecting our rations on a regular basis – initially from Steamer Point, another RAF unit, but, throughout part of August, September and October, we had to collect all rations from the Crater. It was not a nice place to get to, not a nice place to be, and, even harder to get out of – but needs must! From the day we arrived, it had always been the responsibility of a nominated Sergeant to select an airman or NCO to man a bren gun, together with a soldier from the regiment who operated a similar weapon – with one of them at the front of the lorry above the cab, and the other with the bren at the rear. As soon as the lorry left the unit, we would go hell for leather, stopping for nothing or nobody, until we reached the Crater. Once we had loaded up the rations and were clear to leave, we would do the same on the return journey. It was a hairy duty and not one to look forward to. I did my stint as an organiser and, believe me, you don't make any friends that way. I also did two runs on the bren. As well as fear, my most enduring memory was being strapped to the side of the vehicle – a little like being in a helicopter harness – without which you certainly couldn't do the job, as you'd probably be on the road after the first corner. We often had problems, but never a fatality, which probably says more about the drivers and, once again, the Argylls, who were nearly always in the right place at the right time. So, as I said at the beginning, there were no more rations to be had because by that time, we couldn't get to the Crater even if our lives depended on it!

The last four weeks seemed terribly condensed. It was a case of work, guard duty, sleep if you could, followed by work. I remember very little detail except that the numbers being fed had reduced considerably. People were leaving every day – almost every hour, it seemed. They were clearly trying to get everybody out by the 30th. We now fed people ad-hoc: if you came in, you got fed – either by what we had placed in the servery or we just cooked something. We tried to maintain mealtimes, but it became impossible. So, we just kept the servery full of food the best we could, so there was always something available. We were using a lot of 'ten-men' packs during November to supplement the few fresh rations we had left. The packs provided 10 men with three meals – breakfast, dinner and tea. They were pretty basic menus, but we had few food critics.

My one enduring memory from those last few weeks was of the Egyptian staff, who had been so loyal. Almost every minute of every day, someone would beg you to take them to England. They would grab your hands and arms and kiss your fingers, the backs of your hands or your arms – always with the same plea. "I always loyal, Effendi – you take me England or me dead!"

Most people, me included, just smiled and moved on, knowing full well that they wouldn't be leaving. They thought we had the power – we knew differently. I am still haunted by some of those who wept with fear the nearer it got to withdrawal time. The final prediction for my departure happened. I was to leave on W-4, 26th November, 1967. I was informed the day before that I must be outside my accommodation at 07.00 hrs on the 26th. I was only allowed one small pack, which had to be carried – everything else was to be left behind. The reason soon became clear.

There were about 40 of us in my group. We were guided down the 'corridor' between the buildings, heading towards the runway. We could hear sporadic firing, but it didn't seem to be at us. When we reached the runway, we were herded together by our guide who informed us of what was going to happen and what we had to do. Apparently, the aircraft would land further up the runway and taxi towards our position almost at walking pace. After a signal from our guide, we would

RAF KHORMAKSAR, ADEN

run towards the aircraft at about five second intervals, with just a touch on our shoulders being the order to run.

So, it was that the plane came in to land, and was almost at a standstill about a hundred yards from us. The noise of gunfire was everywhere and overpowering, but I found out later that it was us firing at the enemy to ensure they kept their heads down to give us the opportunity to board and give the aircraft time to turn around and get airborne again. By the time the guide touched my shoulder, the aircraft was slightly past my position and about 150 yards away. We had been informed that you could access the plane from a side door or up the rear ramp – in any event, you threw your pack in first and then you were assisted by people pulling you aboard. I chose the ramp. Once aboard, we were told to sit on the floor with our backs to the fuselage, knees bent, hugging our packs. Within what seemed like minutes, the aircraft had turned and was screaming down the runway to gather enough speed to get airborne. Although we could still hear gunfire, it didn't seem to be at us and it was receding fast – so, once again, we were in debt to the Argyll and Sutherland Highlanders.

As I settled down on the floor, now buckled to the side of the aircraft, I glanced around at my fellow escapees only to realise that we were all looking around at one another. Those we knew, we nodded to, but whenever our eyes met there was a smile, whether the person was known to us or not. With hindsight, I believe these were smiles of relief at just being able to share with others the fact that you had got away unharmed.

The journey was uneventful, but after about two hours, we were informed that we were to land in Bahrain! How ironic! I'm not sure why I was surprised – but I was. I think that I thought we were heading for the UK, which in retrospect was pretty stupid, and perhaps, wishful thinking. What was happening was that the aircraft was scooping up as many as they could from Khormaksar, without stopping and endangering the aircraft, then dropping their 'cargo' off at the nearest British-controlled airfield – Bahrain – and then returning to collect more, so that with several aircraft constantly to-ing and fro-ing, all personnel would be out of Khormaksar by the 30th November, 1967. W-Day.

Bahrain was absolutely manic! There must have been thousands of us there. The drill was simple though: we were allocated a bed space in a tent, issued with warm clothing, i.e. long trousers for those, like me, who had left in shorts and a thick service jumper, because it was winter in the UK. Every day, we reported to a central point and, if your name was on the list, you were leaving for the UK. Most of this time, for me, is a blur. I was in Bahrain for about seven or eight days. What did I do? How did I spend my days? I have absolutely no recollection. I only know that on the 3rd or 4th December, my name was on the list, so, gathering together my few possessions, I boarded a transport aircraft for home.

CHAPTER 3

RAF BIGGIN HILL

We arrived at RAF Brize Norton where we were accommodated, given extra warm clothing and eventually transported back to our parent units – in my case, Biggin Hill. Again, most of this is a blur, but I arrived back at RAF Denbury on the 9th December, 1967. I do remember that I travelled the last stretch under my own steam by train to Shrewsbury.

It was an incredibly emotional reunion with the family. Although we had only communicated by letter and clearly I hadn't told Ann about the problems in Khormaksar, towards the end, the newspapers had been full of it and, of course, they're never short on detail! We just never got enough of each other after I got home. We kissed, hugged and made love almost in one continuous flowing motion. The children, of course, were back to normal within 48 hours, although, in my absence, they had become a little wilder and more defiant, all of which was normal with one parent being away. But Ann and I just couldn't leave each other alone. Every spare moment, if we found ourselves on our own, we would make love at any time or in any place. We did, after all, have five months to catch up on! I lost all concept of time.

One morning, a corporal knocked on the door of our married quarter and asked if I would report to the W/O in the General Office as soon as possible. So, that afternoon, I popped in and asked for the Warrant Officer, who, with a smile on his face, informed me that I'd been absent without leave for three days! I apparently had been given seven days leave upon my return from Khormaksar and was then supposed to return to RAF Biggin Hill. I had now been back 10 days! As I said, I had lost all concept of time. I had absolutely no idea how long I'd been home. He was still smiling when he said, "Not to worry" – that he'd informed Biggin Hill that the station had extended my leave period for personal reasons and that now Christmas and New Year were looming, there was little point in my returning until the station reopened on the 8th January, 1968. Apparently, they were more than happy with that – particularly as I was now surplus to requirements – my earlier position as a Corporal Cook had already been filled, so I was now a surplus Sergeant.

As it turned out, none of this was terribly surprising. Thousands of us had returned from the Middle East part way through a tour that should have been completed somewhere else – in my case, Bahrain.

Spike got away from Khormaksar two days after me, i.e. at W-2. We didn't really see each other until sometime during Christmas when Ann and Jane had arranged for the two families to get together for a drink and a snack at their house. Jane had told Ann that she was very worried about Ian (Spike) and that he'd become very withdrawn and wouldn't or couldn't talk about Khormaksar and was saying that he wanted to leave the RAF. It was clearly a difficult time for him and, predictably, in trying to avoid any discussion about Khormaksar, in fact, he had to avoid me. So we didn't actually speak about our experiences in the Middle East until about 36 years later! And, yes, he did leave the Air Force, in October 1968 and emigrated to Australia.

I left Ann and the boys at Denbury whilst I returned to Biggin Hill. That was hard, having been away for so long and it was difficult for the younger boys to accept that this would be only for a short while. In fact, just long enough to find a house. I left with a heavy heart, amidst floods of tears, on Sunday 7th January, and arrived at Biggin at 20.00 hrs. This was my first experience of staying in a Sergeants' Mess. What a difference! It was everything I had expected – the private room, albeit not en suite – someone to greet you at the reception, then talking to you as though you were a guest at a hotel and directing you to the bar, the ante-rooms, the snooker room, the dining room … A batman even carried my case up to my room and said that if I wanted my shoes cleaning, just to leave them outside my door when I retired. Dixie Dean had arrived!

The following morning, I reported to the General Office to start the arrival procedures. I was told that the Warrant Officer who was in charge of the Station Services Flight, which included all the administration and pay for the station, wanted to see me. What a difference a rank made! He shook my hand and invited me to sit down. He spoke to me as though we were equals – we were, after all, members of the same club! With hindsight, I now believe that his courteous attitude had a lot to do with where I'd come from, i.e. the Middle East. Nevertheless, that short meeting, together with another with his opposite number at Denbury, altered my view of SNCOs and Warrant Officers from that day forward. Gone were my jaundiced views of W/O Pocock, the Station Warrant Officer at Denbury, Flight Sergeant Hanrahan and Sgt. Magin, all of whom ruled over me in the Airmen's Mess at the same station. They, and others, had laid the foundation of my hatred and contempt for authority and for what I thought of as the injustices of the system. I had finally grown up.

The reason behind this particular little chat with the Warrant Officer was to tell me that, because I had served less than six months in the Middle East, I was still on the unaccompanied overseas list and would quite likely be called upon to complete another tour – and because I was now excess baggage at Biggin Hill, it was likely to be within the next 12 months. Well, I was absolutely flabbergasted – I was almost speechless.

"That is so bloody unfair," I heard myself saying. I could feel the heat rising in me and I knew an explosion was imminent. Unfortunately, it would have been aimed at this very pleasant, polite Warrant Officer.

Almost as though he could sense this explosion coming, he held up his hand in a gesture of peace and quickly said, "However, there may be a way around it." Keeping his hand in the peace gesture, he went on to say, "How would you feel about an accompanied tour?"

The question hung in the air for a few seconds. He then went on to say that, because I had been back from Singapore for over two years, I was eligible to apply for another accompanied tour. I think I was kind of dumbstruck!

"Would it work?" I asked. "Are they likely to overlook my shortened unaccompanied tour for another accompanied one?"

"I don't know," he said, "but you have completed nearly five months in Aden and they are still looking for personnel for accompanied tours. I will write a recommendation on your behalf for the Station Commander, so I think we have got a better than 50% chance." He smiled. "Do you mind where you go? I don't think you want to be too picky!"

I smiled back. "No, anywhere, as long as it's accompanied – and thanks!"

"Okay," he said. "Leave that with me. Now I suppose you had better arrive!"

This could have been a difficult period for us as a family. It was the worst kind of limbo. But Ann, as usual, stayed positive. The following weekend, having travelled back to Denbury, I recounted all that had been said in this meeting, to a very happy and relieved Ann.

"It sounds great," Ann said. "Everything will work out fine. In the short term, all you have got to do is find us a house, so we can be together and you don't have to travel back here every weekend."

So, that's what I did. Within a month, I had located a nice little bungalow in Biggin Hill village, which the powers-that-be agreed to accept as a hiring. A hiring was a privately owned property whose owners agreed to rent to the MOD for an agreed sum of money. The resident, in this case me, paid exactly the same rent as for a married quarter and all the same conditions applied. All of the contents were held on an inventory that was checked and signed for and subject to inspection when you handed it back. The only slightly tongue-in-cheek difference with this particular inventory was that the owner insisted that his 48 rose bushes were included! I signed anyway, and was so pleased to have the family all together again. Ann absolutely fell in love with the place. It was a picture-postcard bungalow right in the heart of the village within a five-minute walk to the infant school for the two eldest boys.

Having arrived back at Biggin Hill, I ended up as a Second Sergeant back in the Airmen's Mess, really just doing exactly what I'd been doing as a Corporal, but on day shifts, from Monday to Friday, which was great, as it gave me the weekends off.

That was an absolutely wonderful spring and summer. We bought a Humber Hawk from an Admiral Sir Charles Little, which was advertised in the Sergeant's Mess. The asking price was £200 o.n.o., but you had to collect it from Chatham Docks, which I did, with the help of a friend who drove me there. It was huge. Six or eight people could travel in it quite comfortably. It also had a pull-down cocktail cabinet in the back – for the use of the passengers. Its only downside was that it only did about 20 miles to the gallon – a gallon of petrol back then was the equivalent of 27p today – but it would only get used at weekends anyway as I'd got a bicycle for the two miles to work. We finally settled on £180.00 for the car, so all I had to do was insure it! Oh, and get a driving license. I did the latter four months later, but I never got around to insuring it! Ho hum!

Just about every weekend through that spring and summer, we were out somewhere – it was absolutely wonderful. Could life get better than this? Yes! On the third of August, I was informed that *we* would be leaving for Cyprus on 15th October, 1968. To say that Ann was ecstatic would be an understatement. Not only was it an accompanied tour, but Ann's elder brother, John, had been in Cyprus for the better part of ten years, serving with the Engineers in the British Army. They can get longer tours than the RAF.

So, we started again. I ordered deep-sea boxes – this time eight smaller ones, remembering the problems we'd had previously with larger boxes. (If they are too heavy to lift, they are more likely to be dropped!) We had now accumulated some furniture which we arranged to have stored in Ramsgate, near my mother's house. With summer now almost behind us, it was rush, rush, rush. Two and a half months soon fly by when you are preparing to move to another country. But Ann, as always, was brilliant. By the middle of September, all the boxes had been packed and were collected for shipment, with a lot of help from three excited children. It wasn't really worth it, but we sent the eldest two back to school for the remaining month. It just gave us a little more freedom to tie up all the details of our move. I sold the Humber to a junior officer in Station HQ for £150.00 and, before you knew it, the bus arrived to take us to RAF Brize Norton for the next stage of our adventure. We had been at Biggin Hill less than eight months!

CHAPTER 4

RAF EPISKOPI CYPRUS

Twelve hours later, we arrived at RAF Akrotiri a little tired, but excited. We were then bussed to Limassol, which was about six to seven miles away and there, with many others, we booked into a hotel for the night. We were informed by a young officer, prior to going to our rooms, that we should congregate the following morning at 10.00 hrs in the large ante-room for an arrival briefing.

The whole episode of packing and moving seemed to have finally caught up with Ann. She seemed rather listless in the morning and said that she was still very tired, so this was one of the few occasions that I took over. She didn't want any breakfast, so we left her in bed to catch up. I dressed the boys and the four of us went down for breakfast and then onto the meeting at 10.00 in the ante-room.

During breakfast, Ann's brother, John, arrived. He had taken the day off to help find us a house. I explained about Ann and suggested that he catch up with her later in the day when she was more rested. The briefing was pretty predictable. "Remember you are in a foreign country, so be courteous …" and, "Although this is October, the temperature will still climb to about 28 to 30 degrees centigrade, so be careful …" and so on.

"You can stay in the hotel for up to 14 days, courtesy of the MOD, but it is anticipated that you would have found a house by then!"

The system of finding a house was fairly simple, made more so because we had John as a guide. I booked in at the Housing Agency, which was in Limassol, who informed me what we could afford, based on my rank and then they gave me a selection of houses to look at. After that, it was just a case of bartering with the landlord! John's wife, Stella, offered to look after the children whilst John and I looked at properties. Although Limassol is a large, sprawling town situated on the southern coast of the island, we were limited as to where we could live. There were large areas taken over by the Turkish community and equally large areas taken over by the Greeks. Most of the houses that were available to the British military were within a few miles of the main road, which was called the By-Pass. The By-Pass sort of cut Limassol in half, running from the Mediterranean at your back in the direction of Akrotiri which was sort of south/south-west. So, all of the military facilities were also in that area, i.e. the NAAFI, medical/dental services and a centre of information which also contained the Housing Agency. It was also where we picked up the transport to the two main RAF units – RAF Akrotiri and my unit, RAF Episkopi – which were both about the same distance from Limassol.

With an awful lot of John's help, we looked at four houses that day and finally chose a lovely detached bungalow with a huge grapevine on the roof. It was near an area called Curium, which was at the bottom of the By-Pass and about a 15-minute walk from the sea and shops. The bungalow also had 12 lemon and orange bushes and an abundance of colourful plants in the garden. I was sure that Ann would love it.

At about 15.00 hrs, John and I collected Ann from the hotel, who was now much more her old self. After about 15 minutes of tears, because she had not seen her brother, John, for several years due to his service commitments, we then took her to see what would be our home for the next three years and she fell in love with it on sight! That night John, Stella and their family – Christopher, who was four-years old, and Sharon who was the same age as Tony, seven-and-a half – took us all to their favourite restaurant in the Turkish quarter called Niazzi's for our first kebab, and to taste what was to become our favourite wine, Kokinella, a plump, sweet red, but potent concoction, which was free with every meal! That night set the standard for hundreds of family meals yet to come.

The following day, which was a Thursday, John, Ann and I returned to the Housing Agency. Stella had kindly offered to look after the children again. They confirmed that the house was fine and that we could move in as soon as we liked. They also confirmed that I was to report to the Station HQ at RAF Episkopi on Monday 21st October to begin arrival procedures. So, having dropped Ann off at John and Stella's house, John and I went about the laborious business of taking over the inventory of the bungalow. It was not so different to taking over a married quarter in that it was fully furnished and fully equipped – even down to the pruning shears for the grapevine! By 17.00 hrs, it was all done. The landlord, whose name was Georgio, followed by an unpronounceable surname, lived next door, which proved really useful during the first few weeks. He was also an extremely nice person, as was his wife Maria, who spoke no English at all!

We collected Ann and the children from John's house and, having promised to meet the following day about the same time for another kebab at Niazzi's, we settled into our new house. After shopping at the NAAFI which was about a 20-minute walk away, and a quick bite to eat, we tucked in three exhausted, but excited children (Andrew was particularly so) and retired to sit on our balcony, which ran the whole length of the front and down one side of the bungalow. In the dying embers of the day – it was about 21.00 hrs – it was still pleasantly warm and, as we clinked our glasses together, we looked out at one of the most unspectacular views I have ever seen – a 'bondu,' a piece of waste ground, covering an area of about 50 square yards – but, with all the lights twinkling from the street and surrounding houses, it looked magical to us.

"Happy?" I asked. Ann smiled back, as only Ann could smile and said, "I don't think I've ever been happier."

The following week just whizzed by, although the Information Centre in Limassol had told me that from Monday 21st we changed from summer dress, i.e. KD (khaki drill) to winter dress, i.e. battle dress. At the bus stop, there was a mixture of both. I wore blue. The following week was purely domestic. Ann registered the eldest two at the British School, which was about a 10-minute walk away. She wasn't going to part with Andrew until she had to – which was the following June when he was four. I arrived at the unit and met my Catering Officer – Flight Lieutenant Granville who was due to go home in two months' time. A pleasant, laid-back sort of character, he welcomed me to the Flight and informed me that I would be taking over the Officers' Mess kitchen. I was quite happy about that. Having kicked my heels for eight months at Biggin Hill, I was up for the challenge.

Unlike my arrival at Khormaksar, I wasn't confronted with loads of rules and lots of 'dos' or 'don'ts'. The Flight did get together a couple of times a year for a meal and so on, but that was organised by the W/O in the Airmen's Mess and there didn't seem to be any three-line whip.

In short, it was a smallish Flight, probably of about 60 to 70 military personnel, with a similar number of civilians made up of Turkish and Greeks (although they were mostly Turkish). However, the Officers' Mess did have a small number of Sudanese staff waiting in the bar, dining room and officers' accommodation. They were lovely people who all lived together in, what was aptly named, the Sudanese Lines. In the years to come, Ann, myself and the boys, along with several other Officers' Mess staff and their families, spent some really wonderful, memorable days at the Sudanese Lines – the Sudanese are a naturally gregarious people who absolutely love children. We formed some lasting friendships there. It was quite often the place we all ended up, at least once a week, usually the weekend! In some ways, most of our UK friendships were formed at the Sudanese Lines. What we all had in common was having young children.

I always think of this tour as a turning point in our lives. Although it turned out to be a very busy job in the Officers' Mess, with about four or five royal visits, which included Princess Margaret, a couple of duchesses, a prince and one or two other foreign nobles, if I remember correctly, as well as what seemed like an overload of 'in-house' functions, simply because we were overseas and seem to have more free time – well, the officers did, anyway.

In any event, as I have said, it was a very busy job, supported by one of the best teams of chefs I have ever had the pleasure to work with – three corporals, a couple of airmen and three outstanding and loyal Turkish chefs. My success there is only a reflection of how good they were. And, over and above all that, there was my good and loyal friend, Demetrious Christofi, my Greek storeman, clerk, book-keeper and resolver of all problems. Hell, he even looked after our grapevines at home!

Going back to Princess Margaret ... She visited Episkopi in, I believe, 1970. And, of course, there was the usual panic to make sure that everything was perfect – to the extent that they not only repainted the entrance hall and foyer in turquoise – what they were led to believe was her favourite colour – but they also refurnished and repainted a suite of rooms in the same colour, just in case she needed to freshen up, which she didn't! Anyway, whilst they were surveying the entrance hall to see whatever else needed improving, a high-ranking officer stopped by the ladies toilet which, like the gents, was off the entrance hall and said, (I hope quietly), "I can hear someone peeing!" He was inferring, I suppose, that it wouldn't do if you could hear the princess. So, they actually built a wall three feet or so out from the doorway and about five or six feet along so that the ladies loo door was now enclosed! The purpose, I can only guess, was that nobody could get closer than three feet to the ladies' loo door, thereby preventing anyone from hearing her tinkle! And I don't believe she even went in. Ho hum! That, of course, isn't a criticism, just an observation. But worse than that, which gave most of the senior officers apoplexy, she smoked at the table! Off with her head!

There is little doubt in my mind, or Ann's, that Cyprus was a life-changing tour. Once again, like the Singapore tour, my pay increased as a result of the LOA (Local Overseas Allowance), but, unlike Singapore, there were no free house servants – but the increase in pay did go some way towards hiring one, if needed. It also meant that, for the first time, we were able to buy a new car, albeit on hire purchase. I even started up a little private catering business providing parties at home for the officers: dinner parties, barbeques and cocktail parties – that sort of thing – all of which were in great demand, mainly because, for them, it was wall-to-wall socialising and the summer weather lasted eight or nine months of the year! In any event, the rewards of this work purchased us three new cars – not all at once, of course. We started with a Simca 1100cc, graduated to a 1300cc and finally bought a de-luxe Simca 1500cc. But what is a Simca? I hear you ask. Do you know, I haven't the remotest idea, but they were very popular! But what I do know is that I did one or two parties every week for almost three years. It got so busy that I set up a little syndicate with three or four other chefs and it was still difficult to keep up with the demand – especially if you wanted a life!

At the beginning of 1969, as a result of a conversation with one of my Turkish chefs, Gouna, I erected three tents on Evdimou beach, a large one for sleeping, a smaller one as a kitchen and an even smaller one containing an Elsan toilet – the contents of which were buried before we left. We spent every spare moment down on the beach, particularly in the summer months – which, as I've said, in Cyprus is about eight months a year. Gouna owned the land that came right down onto the beach, so he offered to check the tents regularly, just to make sure that they weren't being vandalised – which they never were. I usually erected them in March/April and removed them in the October/November, so we had a beachside holiday home for the best part of nine months a year because the little bay was at the bottom of private land and was marked 'Private,' so nobody else ever used it! Does life really get better than this? The adjoining bay, which was a short swim away, had a number of little beach shops – so, usually with one of the elder boys on my back, we would use an empty five-gallon plastic container as a float, then fill it up with fresh water when we arrived, collect our provisions and then swim back! Beat that for a holiday. And we stayed there for varying periods of time, about 40 times a year!

Incidentally, Evdimou is between Episkopi and Paphos on the south-southwest coast. Although, it's difficult to make comparisons, I believe that the Cypriot tour surpassed all other tours in my 31 years of service. We had no financial problems and, as a result of the beach tents we, as a family, spent more time together than, I believe, would normally happen. Also, a number of our friends pitched their tents alongside us for sometimes weeks at a time, courtesy of Gouna, so we often had company. And although at times, I found it difficult to juggle work, private parties and leisure time with my family, it was somehow managed and I look back on those times as being amongst the happiest of my life.

During the high summer, when the boys had gone to sleep, Ann and I would go skinny-dipping and then lie on the beach wrapped in a large towel and make love. Quite often the boys would wake us up because we'd fallen into a deep sleep. Then she would have to 'shoo' them way whilst she found some clothes – oh, what happy days.

Sometimes, at the height of the summer, usually prompted by John, Ann's brother, we would all go up into the Troodos mountains – which is a large mountainous range about one hour's drive from Limassol. Here, the heat would drop from the 30° to 35°C in Limassol to a very comfortable 24° to 25°C and we would barbeque – well, John would barbeque. He'd been in Cyprus for so long, not only did he speak the language passably well, but he would barter in the little shops at Platres – a small village about half way up the mountains – for the best prices on chicken, meat (usually goat) and sausages for barbequing. He also had an array of equipment to simplify the task. The end result was always wonderful. Barbequed chicken, goat and sausage with fresh salad. And, as the sun was setting, we would make our way back down to Limassol, having escaped the heat of the day.

Also living in Platres were a couple of friends we had made – Andreas and Maria. Andreas was my fruit and vegetable supplier at the Officers' Mess. About once a month, during the summer, a number of us would be invited up to his house for a barbeque. It was always the same. Tables would be set up under his grapevines and they were absolutely laden with salads, cheeses, olives, pitta bread and bottles of beer and wine. A short distance away, his mother sat down in what I always think of as the Chinese fashion – knees up to her armpits with her backside almost reaching the floor, leaning forward over rows and rows of meat on long spikes, cooking over a large bed of coals 'on the floor'. The long spikes of meat – which were usually goat – were resting on V-shaped pegs the length of the fire and, every few moments, she would turn the poles so that the meat was evenly cooked. It always had a very distinctive smell and taste, which ever since, I have associated with our visits to Andreas and which I missed so much when we returned to the UK. It's those occasions, with friends that stay with you forever.

Two events happened towards the end of 1969 – both important, but completely unrelated. The first event was in the November of that year when I began to feel restless regarding my career. I had absolutely no idea why. After all, I had only been a Sergeant for a little over two years, so I was hardly being passed over, and, to be honest, you were rarely promoted mid-tour. Nevertheless, the restlessness continued. Earlier in the year, we had a change of Catering Officer. The old one left for Blighty and was replaced by a Polish officer named Flight Lieutenant Radomski. I had met him on one or two occasions and he was a really nice chap, but I didn't think he was the person I should talk to regarding my restlessness. Flight Lieutenant Radomski, like a number of others who had survived the war, but were now too old to fly, were retrained into other branches in order to serve until their 55th birthday. This is a system that I applaud – they had given their all when the country needed them most. However, because my restlessness was solely about my career, i.e. catering, I wasn't sure that he would have sufficient knowledge to guide me. In any event, also stationed on RAF Episkopi was the Command HQ for catering which was commanded by a Wing Commander and a couple from the lower ranks. I think there was a Squadron Leader and a Flight Lieutenant. Anyway, I rang the Command HQ and made an appointment to speak to the Flight Lieutenant. For the purposes of this book, we will call him Flight Lieutenant Patronising Arse. As I have said, I wasn't really sure why I was restless – I think I just wanted someone to point me in the right direction. He greeted me with a smile and offered me a seat in his office. I explained my unease and my uncertainty in my career path. With that, he held up his hand to stop me talking and said, "You're not thinking about a commission, are you?"

"I don't know," I said. "Am I?"

"No, no, no," he said, "a commission is not the right path for you. You need to take your HCIMA through the Open University."

There was a deathly pause. "And how would that benefit me?" I asked. "And what is a HCIMA?"

"Well," he said, puffing out his chest, "it's effectively a degree in catering. I'm a member, of course," he went on to say. "It took me almost three years, but I am a better caterer for it. No, no, what you should do is take your HCIMA (Hotel Catering Institute of Management Association) through the Open University and, with your knowledge of cooking, leave the RAF and pursue your career in civvy street. I can certainly put you in touch with the Education people to get the ball rolling," he continued.

After a short silence, I said, "But I don't want to leave the Air Force. I want to pursue a career in it."

He pondered that for a little while and then said, "Look, don't take this the wrong way, Sergeant Dean, because it's meant to help. You are an incredibly talented chef and, with the right training, your career outside could take off. But …" he had the decency to hesitate, "you are not the right material to become an officer – you are what is called 'a rough diamond'. And, frankly, no amount of polishing is going to change that. Now, I know you're a little disappointed at the moment, but, by the time you've given it some thought, you'll see I'm right."

I smiled, stood up, gave my smartest salute and said, "Thank you, sir. I'd appreciate any help regarding taking my HCIMA and, incidentally, sir, I hadn't even though about a commission until you mentioned it. Thank you."

With that, I 'about turned' and left his office. To say I was angry would be an understatement – I was absolutely fuming. Not because I thought he was wrong – I probably was 'a rough diamond', but because the arrogant, patronising, puffed-up arsehole couldn't see beyond what was standing in front of him. Like so many, he was a founder member of the 'Them and Us' Club – but, in his arrogance, he had laid the foundation for my future.

When I recounted my interview to Ann later in the day, I was still quite heated. She simply said, "Look, I am quite happy as we are, but, if that's what you want to do, then we will make sure that you get enough quiet time to study!"

And she did just that. For the remaining two years in Cyprus, I set aside 30 hours a week – sometimes on the beach at Evdimou, but mostly in the evenings, if I wasn't working. The learning process was sometimes difficult and often fragmented because of the postal system, but always rewarding. I gained a place at Metropolitan College on a three year OU course of which, after two years and because of returning to the UK, I called what I thought would be, a temporary halt to the proceedings. They gave me a Licentiate pass, with a view to completing the final year within the next two. Alas, that never happened, but I still hold a Licentiate Certificate. Just as important though, is the memory of what Ann and the boys gave up to allow me time to study. And, of course, the two-year study had tempered my restlessness – but not my resolve to further my career.

The second event, the date of which I can be more specific about is December 22nd 1969. It's a date I'm never likely to forget. On the afternoon of that day, the family and myself had been invited to drinks at one of my Corporal's houses – Jimmy and Alma Peters. It was a sort of early Christmas party – all of the guests were Officers' Mess staff and their families. We arrived about midday and it must have been about three hours later when it suddenly went dark, almost as though someone had turned the light of the world off. I looked out of one of the windows which looked towards the sea and it just looked as though a terrible storm was brewing, so I told Ann to get the boys together and that we were leaving. I had no idea why I felt we needed to make haste – but I had the most awful premonition. I apologised to our hosts who also found it difficult to understand that if a storm was on the way, why I just didn't ride the storm out in the comfort of their home! I got everyone in the car – the wind was absolutely howling and it rocked the car from side to side. I drove as fast as I dared and Ann tried to quell the now growing fears of the boys – Andrew was particularly scared. We got home just in time. The winds were now almost impossible to stand up in. It had become so dark it could have been midnight and yet it was just 16.00 hrs.

Having got everyone safely indoors, I looked out of the window towards the house we had just driven from. I screamed to Ann to get herself and the boys under a bed in the furthest bedroom of the bungalow – which she did. I went back to the window … I don't know why I went back – curiosity? Fear? I wondered about my earlier premonition. I looked out of the window and went cold – I was witnessing the Apocalypse. Just then, I felt a small hand slide into mine – it was Tony. The horror on his face has stayed with me always. There was a wall of living matter heading towards us – it was just like watching the end of the world! Just seconds had passed and Tony pointed out that there were birds flying within this wall of matter. I looked and couldn't believe what I was seeing. They weren't birds – they were cars, settees, an assortment of furniture. I grabbed his hand and rushed to the back of the bungalow to join the rest of the family. The noise was now thunderous – like standing beside a roaring aeroplane. We wrapped the boys in our arms and waited for what I was certain was the end. It felt as if two hands had grabbed either side of the bungalow and shook it as though someone was making a cocktail. The bed we were under shot across the room, leaving us exposed. Crockery poured out of the cupboards – furniture smashed against the walls. Everything that was not nailed down was just thrown around – and then, suddenly, it went eerily quiet.

I got up and told Ann and the boys to stay put, and pointing at Tony, I said, "And that includes you." That day, for us anyway, was a day of miracles. The sky was now clear and the light had been switched on again. The 'thing', which I was to find out the next day was a waterspout, was one of six tornados that had hit the southern coast of Cyprus. Three of them ripped Limassol apart. Our particular one, like the others, was approximately 300 yards wide and anything in its path was destroyed. Although at my last glimpse the tornado seemed to be heading straight for us, at the last minute it veered slightly left, just destroying our fence and verandah. It uprooted every tree in the front, took down the grapevines and all of the fence separating us from our neighbours. About one quarter of our neighbour's property was totally obliterated, together with the next house and just about every other house in its path, until it petered out in the outskirts of Limassol. 200 homes were destroyed but, miraculously, only five deaths – but considerably more were injured.

The following morning, Tony woke with a white and grey patch of hair, about the size of a half crown, at the back of his head, which served as a constant reminder of how fragile life can be. Jimmy Peters' home was totally destroyed, but they managed to get safely to a cellar so thankfully there were no fatalities.

We returned to the UK in October 1971, and I was posted to RAF Hendon, in north-west London.

CHAPTER 5

RAF HENDON

Our return to the UK, a little like our return from Singapore, was definitely coupled with mixed feelings. Ann, of course, didn't want to return. Life in Cyprus was good. We'd had almost wall-to-wall sunshine for almost 10 months of the year and a much freer lifestyle, partly because of the increase in my pay. We were all in shorts and a little top or T-shirt for most of that time, so we never needed to bundle up against the cold and there was never the necessity or need to stay indoors and keep warm – as I said, this led to a much freer lifestyle. However, as in the case of Singapore, I did want to return, but this time for slightly different reasons. As in Singapore, I had outgrown my job in the Officers' Mess and was definitely looking forward to a new challenge, but more than that, I still had this terrible itch – a feeling that I needed to change direction in my career. I guess I still needed somebody else to confide in, or at least to talk through what was on my mind – besides Ann, of course, who was always 100% behind most of my plans. But, still stinging from my encounter with Flight Lieutenant Patronising Arse, I decided, for the time being, to keep my own counsel.

Being posted to London also came with a housing problem – there were no suitable places for our family – or at least the few left at RAF Hendon were taken, whilst the great majority were being sold off to alleviate the housing problems for civilians in that part of London. So, in the first instance, we were allocated a house at RAF West Malling which was slightly west of Maidstone and south-east of London. West Malling was just a holding unit at that time with little or no function in a military sense, but, like so many RAF stations around London, it had a wartime involvement to be proud of.

Prior to the war, West Malling was mainly used by two private flying clubs, but it had been requisitioned and quickly brought up to speed and tasked as a forward base for Biggin Hill and Henley. The first aircraft to use the airfield were Lysanders. By the September of 1940, West Malling had been bombed five times, suffering varying amounts of damage. It had to close for major repairs and was reopened on the 30th October 1940 when the Spitfires of No. 66 Squadron and the Hurricanes of 421 Flight arrived. By the end of that year though, 66 Squadron had moved to Biggin Hill and 421 to Hawkinge. However, by April 1941, No. 29 Squadron arrived, equipped with Beaufighters. These were used in night operations. One of the pilots with 29 Squadron was Guy Gibson of 'Dambusters' fame.

Whilst the Beaufighters operated at night, West Malling was still used during the day by numerous squadrons as a forward air base. However, as the bombings in Europe intensified, West Malling was used more and more by damaged aircraft that needed to make an emergency landing. Fighters from West Malling also took part in 'diverse' operations – destroying incoming V1 rockets on their way to London. West Malling was considered to be the most successful air base for that task and, to its credit, could claim that it had destroyed 280 V1 rockets! Unfortunately, by August 1944, with the war being fought on mainland Europe and the Nazis in full retreat, West Malling had less of an operational role. It quickly slipped back into its holding role and, with certain variations, remained as such until its final closure in the mid-1970s. Nevertheless, in October 1971, it was still functioning as a holding unit and, as such, it provided housing for those of us stationed in London. It was an absolute pig of a journey getting from that part of the country to RAF Hendon, which was situated north-west of the capital, going towards Stanmore on the Edgware Road, which is, or was, a main arterial road from Marble Arch to all points north.

Following what I thought was a successful tour in the Officers' Mess at RAF Episkopi, it was no great surprise to find that I was back in the Officers' Mess at RAF Hendon. You will remember at the beginning I said that each tour had one or two high points which made them stand out? Well, this tour had four! Unfortunately, three of those were house moves – all inside one year! To be fair, they were all voluntary – always with a view of reducing the travelling time from home to work. Within four months, a house had become available at RAF Northweald, which was about 45 minutes to an hour in the opposite direction – north of London. But, no sooner had we settled down there than I was allocated a married quarter at RAF Uxbridge, which should have been our first destination, but, alas, there were no vacant quarters then. So, having finally settled down and arranged schooling for the children, I could now concentrate on my job as NCO I/C of the Officers' Mess kitchen. Oh, and by the way, did Ann ever complain about any these additional moves? Not a peep! These things she just took in her stride as it was all just part of service life!

The fourth, and probably the most important high point, was the official opening of the RAF Museum by Queen Elizabeth II. I was tasked with providing a luncheon buffet at the Museum for the Queen and her hangers-on – about 80 in all – as well as several other meals, both dinners and luncheons pre- and post-event for the organisers! To be honest, I took most of these events in my stride, having had the benefit of my experience in Episkopi, where I had catered for several members of the royal family – albeit the extended family, a handful of dukes and duchesses. Oh, and one prince (although I think he was foreign) and one countess (and she might have been foreign, too) – and, of course, the Princess Margaret Rose. But I had never catered for the Queen and Prince Phillip before.

Anyway, we can skip over that – suffice to say, it all went according to plan. The highlight for me was that, as we were carrying up the food to where the buffet was being held, which was a sort of servants' stairway, who should be in front of us, cursing and swearing for all to hear, even allowing for the calming tones of his lovely wife? None other than Group Captain Douglas Bader! Apparently, he'd chosen to use the servants' stairway because the steps were wider and shallower, so it was clearly easier for him to throw up each leg to ascend. Although, to this day, I don't know why he hadn't just used the lift! I can only suppose it must have been broken. I looked at Mrs. Bader, hoping that my eyes were saying, "Can I be of help?" She clearly understood and gave me a little smile and a small shake of her head. You didn't 'help' Group Captain Bader!

I have to say though, that, other than the Museum opening, Hendon, for me, was almost a non-tour, although I found the job, at times, challenging. By the spring of 1973, we were on the move once again though – this time to the Command Headquarters at RAF Brampton in Huntingdonshire.

CHAPTER 6

RAF BRAMPTON

This move was, in a family sense, less troublesome than some. Within a month of arriving, we were allocated a married quarter, so the separation from my family was kept to a minimum. As was fast becoming my hallmark, it was no great surprise to find that I had been tasked with taking over the Officers' Mess kitchen. There were two Officers' Messes at Brampton. The important one for me was the Command Officers' Mess. This mess was much busier and dealt with all visitors to the Command HQ, so there were many high-powered luncheons and dinners for some very influential people. With one eye still on my career, I was aware that this was one job, that if done right, could place me in the spotlight! But, you know what they say, 'be careful what you wish for'! More of that later.

This was a tour that stands out in my memory. Firstly, Ann decided to get back into the workplace. She applied for and gained a position as a clerk in the Civil Administration Department on the unit. She was absolutely delighted, albeit a little nervous. This would be the first time she had worked, other than as a mother and housewife, for nearly 14 years. But, being naturally bright and with above average written and numerical skills, she soon settled in. However, just the result of this change was quite dramatic. Not only did we have to rethink our day, but we all had to pull together. The children weren't babies any more – Andrew, the youngest, was just approaching eight years of age, with Tony, the eldest, being 12. Organising the household became a bigger chore after Ann returned to work, but, between us, we still managed to run the family home well.

The change in Ann was even more amazing though. I always wanted the three boys and myself to be able to give her enough freedom to pursue her working life without the day-to-day pressures of cooking, cleaning, shopping and so on, so we set up a roster of jobs that we all had to complete, either individually or collectively and, in the main, this scheme worked. But the change in Ann, for me anyway, made all of the domestic changes worthwhile. She suddenly had a purpose, besides bringing up our family. She was now concerned about something beyond us. She always looked lovely to me, but having to go out to work made her more conscious of her appearance, and she always looked her best when she went off in the mornings. She became a better organiser, fitting her new job in and around her normal domestic day, although, as I have already said, we now all pulled together. She became even more interesting to be with too as she seemed to view things differently now she was at work – it sounds ridiculous, but she seemed more whole in herself. She had never complained once during the previous 13 or 14 years of domesticity, but there was little doubt in my mind that she needed this input, outside of her family life.

Meanwhile, I had settled into my new job and, as predicted, it was busy. However, it was about to become much busier. Within Support Command, of which Brampton was the headquarters, there was a team of staff, chefs, cooks and stewards that were cobbled together to form a royal/diplomatic team of caterers to look after the needs of royal and diplomatic visits or just those of ordinary 'important' people, mostly in London, but really almost anywhere. Rather than burden the nearest RAF station with the sort of work that they would normally be unlikely to come across, our team would be activated.

My involvement started in October 1973. Apparently, they were short of a chef and my name came up. I was invited to attend a meeting at Brampton HQ, which was led by the officer responsible and the team leaders – namely, a Flight Sergeant Chef together with a Flight Sergeant Steward. I have purposely avoided giving them names, mainly because it's unnecessary and I'm not in the business of pointing fingers. This particular meeting was to organise a luncheon that was to be held in London for a member of a European royal family, a number of MPs and several high-ranking military people, the total number being 18. I was only really invited to attend the meeting, I thought, because I was the 'new boy' and the meeting was being held at RAF Brampton, my home station. In reality, I was just a member of the team, working directly under the Flight Sergeant, so would not normally have been invited or involved in the planning. Nevertheless, I was there and, for some unknown reason, this seemed to agitate the Flight Sergeant who clearly thought I was there to offer advice and I guess he felt that his position as team leader was being assailed! This couldn't have been further from the truth and the team were told so by the officer in charge, but he went on to suggest that, with my background, I might just be able to offer something of value.

However, and this is a big 'however'… there was an element of truth in his comment. The menus for these events can be agreed by one or two methods. The 'chef' submits three menus to the office of the Command Catering Officer, who will, in turn, select a menu that they think appropriate or we can be informed by the 'aide' of the visiting diplomat about a preferred item and then build a menu around it and forward this on for approval through the Command Catering Officer. In this particular case, the second option happened. Apparently, the royal member had requested chicken Kiev as a main course.

A couple of years earlier, resulting from something I learned in Singapore, I wrote an article for the *Catering News* on an alternative and, I thought, risk-free way of producing chicken Kiev. In my opinion, the hardest thing to create in chicken Kiev is that moment when the diner cuts into the chicken and out flows the garlic butter. In my experience, and often to my shame, what normally happens is there is only a nicely flavoured, but rather dry chicken. The normal procedure for producing chicken Kiev is to remove the breast, retaining the small wing bone for presentation, slicing along the length of the breast with a sharp knife after removing the skin and then filling the cavity with garlic butter, before closing the two halves together and then dipping it in flour, beaten egg and breadcrumbs so it can be deep fried. Now, if you are preparing just one or two, there is no reason why this method shouldn't work. But, and it's a big but, if you are preparing the same item for any number over say four to six, this method is open to problems. There are just too many variables, mainly during the cooking process, but not exclusively. I also believe that the whole procedure is open to question. The fat has to be at just at the right temperature, for instance, so, if too many are added at once, the fat cools – therefore, by the time the chicken is cooked and is of a presentable colour, the chances are that the butter will have leaked. And if you cook a few at a time, the majority will have spent too much time on a hot plate waiting for the last few to be presentable – and the results are usually the same: dry chicken. The secret is to get the chicken out of the fat, place it on your salver, decorate it with a little chef's hat on the small wing bone and get it out to the diner!

My method takes longer in preparation but is foolproof – it will leave the diner wondering how on earth the chef can have produced something of such quality for so many. It involves removing the breasts from the chicken, including the little wing bone and all the skin. Inside the breast, you will find a fillet that runs the length of the breast – remove this carefully. Using a damp cloth to cover the breast and fillet and then beat them carefully with a wooden mallet until each are about three times the size. Place your garlic butter on the expanded fillet of chicken and roll it up, tucking in the edges. Now place your little parcel onto the widest part of the chicken breast and, starting furthest from the point, roll it up, tucking in the sides and pin the join with cocktail sticks. Now, instead of using flour – as in flour, egg and breadcrumbs – use rice flour or cornflour, preferably rice flour. Set the Kievs on a tray with the joint down and wing bone pointing up and leave them in a fridge overnight. The following morning, remove them from the fridge, take out the cocktail sticks, dip them in beaten egg and finally breadcrumbs. You now have your butter locked into a rice flour shell, which will just become crispier during the cooking process. Ta-da! The perfect Kiev every time, in my opinion anyway.

Nevertheless, even having proven the case in my kitchen, the powers that be were assured by the Flight

Sergeant that the former problem I had highlighted wouldn't happen. He also argued that my preparation time was too lengthy and that the final presentation of his chicken Kiev would look more appealing. His last point was bullshit! Unfortunately for him, the outcome was a disaster. I think, with hindsight, he tried too hard to make his point. Several Kievs opened during the cooking process and, of course, made a mess in the fryer, which, in turn, burnt onto the outside shell of the other chicken pieces. Unfortunately, no amount of decoration could disguise the finished article. I felt bad about it – we all felt bad about it. We were, after all, a team. A week later, I was called up once again to the Command HQ to be informed that the Flight Sergeant had stood down and its new leader was me.

Staying on the catering theme for just a little while, the next large function for the team was a luncheon at Admiralty House in London for the then Force's Minister, who was Roy Mason. The officer in charge of this particular function was none other than Squadron Leader Fenton of RAF Khormaksar fame. In view of our past history, I wasn't expecting an easy ride, but to be fair, other than raising his eyebrows and a particularly hard handshake, he went on to say that it was nice to see me again. Apparently, the menu had been produced (I assumed by him) and presented as a *fait accompli*. The main course was saddle of lamb! Now, saddle of lamb can be any chef's nightmare – especially if it's being produced in a strange, untried kitchen.

"Why saddle of lamb?" I asked offhandedly.

"Because it suits the occasion," he replied, more pointedly. "And why not?" he continued, clearly not willing to brook any argument.

"Oh, no real reason, sir. Except, as you know" – and I wasn't sure he did – "saddle of lamb can be a nightmare if you're not used to the ovens or they're too small or in the wrong place. Have you had the opportunity to check the kitchen, sir?" I asked.

"Oh, you have no worries there, Sarge," he responded. "Admiralty House has two fully equipped kitchens. There is a small, but fully equipped one on the floor where the function is being held, and there's a much larger one on the floor beneath which caters for all the personnel who work at Admiralty House."

I pondered this. "How many are we catering for, sir?"

"Oh, between 18 and 20 – the figure's yet to be confirmed," he said.

After a few more minutes of silence, I said, "So you think that the kitchen on the function floor will meet our needs?"

"Yes, yes," he said. "You may have to do a bit of juggling, but I'm sure you're up for that, aren't you?"

"Yes, of course, sir. If you're happy?"

"Yes, yes, of course I'm happy. Remember, sometimes we have to adapt and, if the worst comes to the worst, you can always use the main kitchen below!"

"Adapt. Right, sir. I can do that."

So why did I still feel uneasy? In order to put things into perspective, the reader needs to know that normally when you arrive at these venues you have to be totally prepared. These venues are not next door or even close to a supermarket or, indeed, any form of grocery outlet where you can put right a mistake or replace a forgotten item. Nothing can change the menu! You are literally stuck – you put right anything that might go wrong. However, logistics are the problem for the organisers. Food was my problem – so, I decided on three saddles. I would normally expect to feed seven to 10 diners off one saddle. But with the numbers still unconfirmed, but being somewhere between 18 and 20, it was better to err on the side of caution. The starter and dessert were simple enough on paper, as long as there was sufficient room to lay out a possible 20 plates for the hors d'oeuvre which was 'timbales de salmon en d'ecrivesses', to which I also liked to add a little minced crab. The hors d'oeuvre would be made at Brampton, and I would also make syllabub, the desert, there. The sauce that he had decided should accompany the saddle was a 'reforme' sauce, which is normally associated with cutlets, but was not necessarily incorrect. Made correctly, the reforme sauce starts its life as a simple brown sauce (espagnole) to which you add tomato sauce, sherry, chopped onions, carrot and minced raw ham. Simmer and strain and you have got sauce poivade (pepper sauce). This is the sauce that I would take to London. Then, all I needed to add was port wine and redcurrant jelly to produce the reforme!

48 hours before the event though, I was still a little concerned about the cooking of the saddles and because

we still had an unconfirmed dining number, I decided to ring the kitchen at Admiralty House. The chef was helpful but, I sensed, very busy. However, he did confirm that the cooker in the small kitchen would be inadequate to cook the saddles, but that he was quite happy for me to cook them in his kitchen (the main kitchen) where he would allocate me sufficient space in his large draw plate oven which would accommodate all three.

I left for London with two other chefs and four stewards – including the Flight Sergeant Mess Manager and enough equipment and food to meet the needs of a squadron. We left at 06.30 in order to avoid as much of the London traffic as possible. By 08.30, we had unloaded and moved into the function rooms. From this point on, it was a catering horror story. The function suite was situated on the top floor of Admiralty House, the implications of which I initially hadn't realised. In order to access the top floor from the ground, you have to exit the lift on the second floor, walk the length of the building, where a number of security personnel were visible, and then enter another lift to take you to the top. This is purely a security device so that nobody can access the important and vulnerable areas of the top floors.

The function room kitchen was a trifle tight and there was very little preparation area, as some of the space was required by the stewards and – horror of horrors – the cooker was a domestic model! I began to then think seriously about the menu. Clearly, the saddles would have to be cooked in the main kitchen, but, with only four gas rings (at least they weren't electric), I had to think seriously about the logistics of the accompanying dishes. The Squadron Leader wanted the saddles served with noisette potatoes, asparagus hollandaise and Vichy carrots. None of which would normally be a problem, but with only four rings and a small oven, this was virtually impossible! The only consolation was that the small kitchen had a reasonably sized hot cupboard so, even allowing for space to keep the plates warm, I realised I should still be able to keep some food hot in there. There was also a fairly large refrigerator.

Lunch was set for 13.00 hrs, so we had just about four hours to get ready. I set the other chefs to work on the preparation of the vegetables and all the garnishes required, which I had decided for the saddles would just be small turned vegetables, i.e. potatoes, carrots, turnips and swede, which were to be boiled and placed around each saddle, just to give it a little colour, together with some watercress, and vegetables to be no bigger than one inch. This was time consuming to prepare, but worthwhile. For the timbale, three small lettuce leaves were taken from the heart of the lettuce. A small finely diced salad of cucumber, tomato, celery and potato was to be decorated with slices of anchovy, capers and chopped aspic. Also, I had to set out all the ingredients for the syllabub and the hollandaise sauce. I had prepared 25 timbales back at the unit (just in case) and they were now in the fridge. So, other than turning them out (which is done in warm water – just to release the aspic), together with the salad and mayonnaise sauce, I knew the first course should be trouble free!

Satisfied that we were now underway, I decided to introduce myself to the chef in the main kitchen and ask him if I could put the saddles in his fridge ready for the oven – ours definitely wasn't big enough. The response to my first inquiry on the function suite floor regarding the whereabouts of the kitchen was, "Down there!" with the man pointing in the general direction. That I already knew, so I asked him, "Where down there?" He said he thought it was in the basement, but he wasn't sure and told me to ask at reception on the ground floor. I had one of those moments when everything I had dreaded was coming true. In the deep recesses of my mind, I had suspected something like this would happen, but I couldn't bring myself to really believe and act on this fear. Kitchens in large houses are always in the basement and Admiralty House was a very large house! I did ask directions, but I was absolutely seething, with both myself and Fenton, for not checking the facilities before creating the menu – but mostly with myself for trusting Fenton and not following through with my instincts. The golden rule in my industry is, after all, "Leave nothing to chance!"

I found the kitchen and, as I suspected, it was in the bowels of the building. Who said logistics wasn't my problem? I introduced myself to the chef in the main kitchen and explained the problem. The saddles would be required to leave 'my' kitchen at approximately 13.15-13.20. In order to leave nothing to chance, if one man carried one saddle from the main kitchen to the function kitchen, it could take up to 15 minutes – and there was a further 15 minutes needed to remove the loins from the saddle and to slice them and place them back on the saddle for presentation. So, a plan of action slowly built in my mind to get the hors d'oeuvre plated by 12.40. The number of guests had now been confirmed at 18 and I was ready to go. I could leave that with the Flight Sergeant Steward and the saddles sitting around for 15 minutes would do them no harm – especially as they would be in the dining room which was much cooler.

Now is probably as good a time as any to tell you how I prepare a very posh sounding 'Petites timbales de salmon en d'ecrivesse'. A timbale mould is a taller version of a dariole mould, which most people have heard of. I lined the inside of the mould with cool aspic, ensuring that a good quantity adhered to all surfaces, leaving a small puddle on the bottom. In that little puddle – which becomes the presentation face of the dish – I decorated it with a star truffle and with something green and red. I tend to use cucumber skin and pimento. I'm trying to create a picture by doing this. I then line the wall of the mould with smoked salmon, making sure a sufficient amount is hung over the top of the mould, in order to fold it back over and 'close' the timbale. Then, I fill up the mould with the mixture of crab, shrimp and finely chopped prawns, which I have mixed together with anchovy paste, béchamel sauce and, for 25 timbales, about three gills of mayonnaise and three gills of aspic, lemon juice, salt and pepper. Fill each mould to the top and flip back over the overhanging smoked salmon, and refrigerate. Serve it with mayonnaise or an accompanying sauce, if necessary. To serve, place lettuce leaves on a plate and have a bowl of warm water ready on one side. Then, dip the mould in the water just long enough to loosen the aspic – it takes seconds – so I can then turn it onto the leaves and present it with the aforementioned salad and chopped aspic and, perhaps, a little chopped parsley. It really is quite a sensational dish.

At 12.45 on that day at Admiralty House, I left the Corporal cook to finish off all the vegetables. The noisette potatoes I had prepared and cooked a little earlier and placed in the hot cupboard. Noisettes are balls of potatoes cut from whole peeled potatoes with a noisette scoop. I like to parboil my potatoes and then cook them on top of the stove in a large sautuese, constantly moving them in butter until they are golden brown. Then I'd add a little parsley and serve. That left the chef to cook the asparagus, which was tied into 20 servings, seasoned and covered with water and butter under a wax paper lid and cooked for about 20 minutes in the oven. Carrots Vichy are sliced carrots covered in water and butter. These need to be cooked gently until most of the water has evaporated and are then tossed in the remaining liquor and served with chopped parsley. They also require some attention, and need to be on top of the stove where we are also preparing the hollandaise sauce.

So, back to 12.40… Myself and the other Corporal cook took off as quickly as possible down the convoluted route to the main kitchen where I had asked the chef to stagger the cooking time of the three saddles for me. Two were to be out at 12.35, giving them about two hours plus, and I was hoping that if he'd kept his eye on them, they should still be pink and moist. I could take the others out 15 minutes later. I can't honestly say anybody noticed us as we dashed in the kitchen because we were just two more frantic cooks at the height of their lunchtime service. But, there they were, two saddles on the side cooling. I caught the eye of the chef, who just gave me a 'thumbs up' and shouted that he would have the other out in about 10 minutes. We threw a tea towel over each saddle and made our way back up to the top floor. Having missed the lift and then having to explain to a security chap who had just come on duty who we were, we finally arrived back upstairs at 12.55. I sent the Corporal back down for the third saddle.

I noticed, with a degree of pride, that the Corporal I had left in the function kitchen had put the remaining vegetables into the hot cupboard and had also remembered to boil the turned vegetables for the saddle garnish and that he was now preparing the hollandaise sauce. Ah - team work!

I quickly poured the juices from the two saddles into a pan and told the Corporal to find a bit of room to reduce it, to make a 'jus-lié' in case the lamb became dry. By 13.10, I had removed the loins from the two saddles, sliced them and put them back on the saddles and placed the turned vegetables around each. I then covered them with a tea towel and placed them in the hot cupboard. By that time, the other Corporal had returned with the third saddle, on which I set to work, leaving the other Corporal to finish off the hollandaise, which was at its trickiest point. Having boiled together butter, milk and flour, this mixture then has to be transferred to a bain-marie to add fresh egg yolks, and whisked like mad – you cannot afford to let it boil. It then needs a squeeze of fresh lemon juice and off it goes!

The Corporal, who had brought up the third saddle, now started to put the vegetables into the serving dishes – the noisette potatoes and carrots then just needed a sprinkle of chopped parsley and, finally, a drop of hollandaise over each portion of asparagus. This created a balance of sauces, together with the reforme, being offered to the diners. Fortunately, I only had to add port wine and redcurrant jelly to the pepper sauce that I'd prepared at RAF Brampton. A quick 'knap' of the reduced residue was drizzled over the sliced lamb and a bunch of watercress was popped at one end and out it went. It was 13.18!

By the time the stewards had served the first two saddles, the third was finished and was leaving the kitchen at 13.22. We were all absolutely shattered, but satisfied that the plan had worked. One of the Corporals offered to start the syllabub, which is a 15-minute job. You just need to mix together sugar, lemon juice, brandy and a drop of sherry. Fresh cream is then added to this mixture and then you slowly fold in the previously beaten egg whites. Finally, you add a little grated lemon rind. Leave the mixture to stand for a little while in the fridge, and you'll find that you a froth forms on the top. All that is left is to then fill brandy glasses about three quarters of the way with the beaten mixture, avoiding the froth, and just before you serve it, spoon the froth on top of each glass.

By 16.00 hours, we were all on our way back to RAF Brampton. The meal had been a success.

During the rest of that tour, there were several more functions, but nothing quite so calamitous. But, other events did happen during that tour – one of which I have always looked back on with deep regret.

Firstly, I received a Commander In-Chief's Commendation for my work at RAF Hendon. Although grateful, I never really understood why – I had in fact laboured harder at RAF Episkopi. Ho hum! Ours is not to reason why. The other interesting event was when I was called up to Command Headquarters and interviewed by a Wing Commander, who shall remain nameless, although, if I was in the business of naming names, I would scream this gentleman's name from the roof tops. He was kind, thoughtful and supportive. He was, indeed, the first officer I had spoken to regarding my future since my interview with Flight Lieutenant Patronising Arse at Episkopi, and he could not have been more different. He felt that I had potential and that I had been 'noticed'. He also went on to say that it was a difficult leap from an SNCO or Warrant Officer to a Commissioned Officer and it wasn't always the right move. However, he felt that I had the potential and, if that was my chosen path, he would be there to guide me. The seeds were sown!

The final event, of note, is the one of which I am still ashamed. Ann, amongst her many attributes, was by any standard, a beautiful woman. She was blessed with high cheekbones, which even as she got older, never altered. Clearly, it wasn't just me who noticed these things. One of her colleagues at work was a budding photographer. He worked, apparently, on an 'ad hoc' basis with a London colour supplement featuring beautiful woman who could advertise products, such as makeup, jewellery and so on, and he had submitted some photographs that he had taken of Ann – mostly, from the waist up. He told her that he wanted to produce a portfolio of photos to submit to this agency and he assured her that work would quickly follow. I have to admit that some of the photos were brilliant, so I reluctantly agreed. All of this was being done either during her working hours – her boss was clearly easy going – or during lunch and other breaks. But, one evening, after the children had gone to bed, Ann said that, if I agreed, he would like to take some photos of her in a nearby wood in assorted underwear (I guess that sort of thing was popular in the early 1970s!) and, that if I was concerned, I could be there.

Well, to my everlasting shame, I exploded and told her that it was never going to happen and that all of the photography must be stopped – and now! She was so upset and accused me of not trusting her – which I denied, of course. We had a blistering row. My argument was that modelling had no place in our lives and that it would require her to stay where we were, when I was due a new posting in three months, and what was she going to do then? Ann finally submitted and said she thought I was right, and that it could become too complicated with us constantly moving. But, the truth is, once again, she had complied to make my life easier and I'm sure she recognised that my outrage was nothing more than jealousy – and she was absolutely right. I couldn't bear the thought of sharing her with another man! That episode says so much more about her goodness and yet so little about mine! We never spoke of it again. The photographer did, however, ring me up at work and expressed his feelings about me and my lack of faith in my wife and that I had ruined an opportunity of a lifetime. I said I was sorry, and I felt that he was probably right.

In July 1974, I was informed that I had been promoted to the rank of Flight Sergeant and I was posted on the 1st September to RAF Henlow (OCTU – The Officer Cadet Training Unit). When I told Ann about the promotion, she was absolutely ecstatic for me and, with hindsight, this put right the problem of the photography. We couldn't have been happier. In the August, I decided that I would pay a visit RAF Henlow, which was only a little further down the A1 towards London. It was late morning and I suddenly realised that I was doing something that I had never done before: I was actually going to introduce myself to the Officer Commanding the Catering Squadron before my reporting date! I'm not sure that I intended to do that when I left home, but now I was absolutely certain. I walked into the Catering Office, incredibly self-assured and asked the Sergeant Clerk if it was possible to say hello to the Catering Officer. I explained who I was and that I was to be posted there on 1st September and that this was just a courtesy call. He raised an eyebrow, but smiled and said that he would check.

Less than a minute later, I was being shown into the Squadron Leader's office. He was a tall, austere looking man with a very serious face. He slowly unfolded himself from his chair, stared me straight in the eye, extended his arm to shake my hand and said, "Welcome, Flight. Have a seat." I was going to correct him about the rank, as I was one month short of being a Flight Sergeant, but decided it would be impolite.

As requested, I sat in the small armchair facing him and, for what seemed like an absolute age, he just stared at me, not saying a word. I began to feel quite uncomfortable and wondered at the wisdom of my unannounced visit and whether my choice of a blazer and flannels was a little too casual. It got almost to the point when I felt someone had to speak, when, with a half-smile playing on his mouth he said, slightly frowning, "Have you ever thought about a commission, Flight?"

I heard myself saying, "Yes!"

"Right! Then that's something we need to look into," he said. "We'll talk again after your arrival!"

I felt that I had been dismissed, so I rose to leave, and as he also rose, presumably to say farewell, he said, "Have you applied for a married quarter yet?"

I replied that I hadn't, but it was something that I needed to do as soon as possible.

He paused for just a moment, supposedly thinking through his next comment. "We have a system at RAF Henlow," he went on to say, "where Warrant Officers and, well, some Flight Sergeants – but, to date, it's been mostly Warrant Officers – can apply for a Type 5 officers' married quarter. We are blessed here with a surplus of junior officers' married quarters." There was silence. "If you were interested I could possibly put a word in for you."

"Well, yes please sir," I said. "I'm sure my wife would be delighted."

"Oh, well that's fine then. Just leave that with me and I should have some news for you by the time you arrive!"

And, with that, he stuck out his hand to say goodbye. "Look forward to working with you, Flight."

"Thank you sir," I said, and with that, I left.

My head was absolutely spinning. Commission! Officers' married quarter! Working 'with' you? I had never worked 'with' my Station Catering Officer before. I had always worked 'for' them! Did promotion to Flight Sergeant make that sort of difference? I couldn't wait to get home and talk all this through with Ann.

We knew that there was a very strict class structure for married quarters on every station – that's assuming that you were ever in a position to get one, which in itself was difficult. Usually, it was a case of too few houses with too many needing them. Nevertheless, what you were allocated was always down to rank, family size and time served. A Flight Sergeant (like me) married with three children and 16 years service – training doesn't count – behind him, was entitled to a Class C married quarter. A Class C was usually a three-bedroomed semi or a terrace house with downstairs carpeting and only rugs in the bedrooms. A Warrant Officer would be entitled to a three-bedroomed detached house, probably a little larger than the Flight Sergeant's, but still without carpeting upstairs, whereas a Junior Officer Type 5 was usually a three or possibly four bedroomed detached house with a garage and carpeting throughout, and a downstairs toilet! These were luxuries way beyond the imagination of any NCO. Your average Warrant Officer would take this elevation in his stride – he was, after all, at the very top of the tree and, if not revered, he was certainly respected by all officers and possibly a little feared by the junior ones. But Flight Sergeants – well, they could easily feel that they had stepped out of their comfort zone.

It didn't help that our nearest neighbour turned out to be a Squadron Leader Medical Officer, but none of this ever bothered Ann! She slipped on the mantle of the officer's housewife almost as though she had been born to it. For my part, though, I initially felt that I was walking on eggshells.

However, what it did do – and did with a vengeance – it made me want the lifestyle! I wanted to live in an officer's married quarter, not as a gesture because there was a surplus, but by right! So when I was confronted with the many challenges – and there were many – I always asked myself, "Do you want to take your family back to a three-bedroomed attached property with no carpeting upstairs"?

With hindsight, I have now come to realise that all of these things were part of a grooming process, which the 'higher-ups' did both consciously and unconsciously. The conscious part was undoubtedly involved in my job as NCO in charge of the Cadet Officers' Mess Kitchen. That position frequently placed me in a position of knowledge concerning the problems of being a cadet and of empathising with those NCOs and Warrant Officers who had also decided to 'cross the line'. I was able to see the problems first hand and often made judgements for myself as to the suitability of some of the NCOs or WOs who were trying to become officers.

CHAPTER 7

RAF HENLOW

I have come to realise that if RAF Episokopi was a life-changing tour, RAF Henlow was the beginning of the completion of that change. I began to take seriously, the Squadron Leader's question concerning a commission. Outside of my job in the NCO I/C Cadet Officer's Mess, I also returned to school to retake both my English Language and English Literature exams, as well as Economics. This was also suggested by the OC of Catering who really became my mentor. He kindly, but firmly, continued to correct my spoken English, my deportment and my appearance and my thin 'spiv-like' moustache was allowed to grow into a more acceptable 'flying officer kite' type moustache, as my mother was so fond of saying. I was playing squash two to three times a week and running 20-25 miles a week. I spent hours poring over the news in broadsheets, like *The Times* and *The Telegraph*.

Through my mentor, I became aware of nuances of behaviour, dress and deportment and I worked out where I was trying to go to, but never forgot where I had come from. All of this work took place with the support and unstinting encouragement of Ann. One year later, in October 1975, I officially applied for a commission in the Royal Air Force. Unbeknownst to me, I was in a competition with 11 other W/O/NCOs for two commissions, one PC (Permanent Commission) and one Branch Commission and these were usually granted to W/O/NCOs over the age of 35, which I was fast approaching. This was the commission that I sought.

By January 1976, I was informed that I had been successful and I was offered a place on the next Squadron to enter the OCTU at RAF Henlow on 15th March 1976. The biggest surprise was that I was to be trained at my home unit, RAF Henlow, whereas I was expecting RAF Cramwell! No matter, it was just another obstacle.

Ann, of course, was brilliant and told me to do whatever I had to do and to come home as often as I could. Luckily, home was four hundred yards down the road! The children thought it was a real hoot that they might see their father 'on parade' as a cadet as they made their way to school! However, this did present a small problem to the powers that be. They felt that they couldn't just leave me at RAF Henlow, working in the Cadet Officer's Mess, knowing that I was to commence training as an officer cadet. So, I was sent on a course to RAF Hereford for, I think, five weeks. The course was called Q (Cat C). It's a course designed to bring certain Warrant Officers 'up to speed' to meet the challenges of running small catering flights on RAF stations, as the role of a Station Catering Officer. The irony of this was, that if I was successful at OCTU, I would have to do a similar course for officers! A further irony was that the Warrant Officer I pipped for the top place on the course was to become the first Warrant Officer in my first command!

I left for RAF Hereford to complete my Q (Cat C) course in early February 1976. It was an interesting, but not difficult, course. However, because I had been selected for officer training, I felt that I should achieve a reasonable pass mark. It was a strange position to be in because many of the others on the course would end up working for me! It crossed my mind if they achieved a higher pass mark than me, it just might be something that would bite me on the bum later! As it turned out, I did come top of the course, with the runner-up being my first future Warrant Officer.

I managed to get home every weekend. The time between finishing the Q (CAT C) course and the start of OCTU had been granted as leave, so I spent as much of the 10 days as I could with Ann and the boys, as well as finalising my own physical and mental training for the start of OCTU.

CHAPTER 8

OFFICER CADET TRAINING UNIT

I had to report to the Cadet Officers' Mess at 16.00 hrs, so I left home at 15.45. It seems rather silly now as I just walked up the road with all the necessary kit and clobber one needs for a 14-week course. My kit was left in a central area until I had been allocated a room. The 16.00 hrs gathering was a 'meet and greet'. An opportunity for the staff to meet the 'hairies,' – a name given to those who crossed over from the rank and file. It was also an opportunity to meet your fellow cadets, both brother hairies and the greater majority who had joined from 'civvy' street or university. Those from other walks of life, other than the service, had all joined two weeks earlier in order to study the drill and bring them up to speed with simple service ways which, for the hairy, had been a way of life. They also received 'knife and fork' course-dining etiquette training!

I approached this gathering with a level of apprehension – I was probably out of my comfort zone. We gathered in the ante-room, a large room adjoining the dining room. Including the directing staff, there were probably about 80 of us. Other than the hairies, everybody else was in uniform, so it was easy to pick out those of us who had just arrived. There were eight of us and none seemed to know each other – I certainly didn't know any of the other seven. The more I walked around and met the other members of my squadron-to-be, the more I realised the difference in our ages. The average age of the hairies was about 37, but the average age of the remaining squadron was about 20! My initial thought was that my extra years just might be an advantage. The bottom line was that in some circumstances or situations they were, but generally, it was a level playing field. They younger ones were generally brighter, better educated, fitter and, more importantly, they were a blank canvas – putty to be moulded. I had the experience of nearly 20 years of service, man and boy. I had the experience of command. I had a wealth of knowledge. However, my one abiding thought, which my mentor had impregnated into my brain, was to use all those tools wisely! To appear to know too much, too soon – to constantly raise one's arm in response to what seemed a simple question by a member of the direction staff or to just to appear to be a 'know all' could quickly work against you. So my plan of action, if one could call it that, was to forget my past, unless it would help others, and to think of myself as a cadet and not a Flight Sergeant – and to never answer back to a member of the directing staff, even though some would have been junior in rank in my former world. I vowed to never be too pushy in group situations unless it helped the whole group and, finally, to be an equal part of the Flight that I was to join – equal in all things. Time would decide my strengths and weaknesses.

My Flight was 'D' Flight in Green Squadron. The squadron was about 80 strong. My Flight consisted of ten members, three female and seven male. During the next 14 weeks, they were the main constituents of my world. We were links in the same chain. All of our thinking was done with each other in mind. You quickly learn that to survive officer training, you must always work as a team. Individuals rarely survive and are quickly ostracised. By 18.00 hrs, accommodation had been allocated and we assembled outside the Cadet Officers' Mess in working dress with boots for a 10-mile run!

Regardless of which uniform we wore, for the next 10 weeks, we always wore boots! It's only in the last few weeks that we were allowed the comfort of shoes. This first hurdle was something that I was aware of – my boots had been 'worn in' since December and I'd been running in them since that time, so they were like slippers to me!

Interestingly, of the 10 in my Flight, two were from the rank and file – myself and one of the girls who was 27 and had been an aircraft loader. Her name was Anita. The remainder either came through university or from a civilian career, with ages ranging from 18-24. Anyway, the point I am trying to make is that, prior to the arrival of the hairies, little emphasis had been placed on physical fitness. Their first fortnight had either been classroom-based or drills, so fitness was left to the individual to sort out or ignore! Also, for the first fortnight, they had been given the option to wear either boots or shoes so, if they weren't careful, they could so easily have been lulled into a false sense of what was to come! To be fair to the directing staff, all the warning signs were there, but at least three in my Flight ignored them. The outcome was extremely sore feet – one fell by the wayside and had to walk back, but all three were in pain – with only boots to look forward to the next day. You will remember my plan of action to forget I was a Flight Sergeant, and think only of myself as a cadet? Well, it was put to the test on our first run. The one who fell by the wayside was one of the female direct entrants, and she fell right in front of me. I stopped, as you do – you know – female in distress and so on. The next thing I know, I've got this Sergeant Directing Staff screaming his head off at me about two inches from my face.

"What the f****** hell do you think you're doing, Cadet Dean? Stand to attention, Cadet Dean. Did I tell you to fall out? Did I tell you to help her? The answer to all the aforesaid is no! So, mind your own bloody business, Dean, and leave her where she is!"

"But …" I said, thinking I might say that she needed help.

His face narrowed the gap between us to about one inch.

"If you utter one more word, Cadet Dean, your 10-mile run will be a 20-mile run! Now, hit the road – before I think you're taking the piss out of me!"

So, I gritted my teeth and hit the road. The first opportunity I got, I glanced back and guess what? The Sergeant was helping her up! Who said chivalry was dead?

Looking back, it's difficult to put the next 14 weeks into perspective. I think of it as an island in my life. One thing is absolutely certain – without the enormous amount of help and guidance I received prior to starting OCTU, together with the love and unstinting support from Ann, who encouraged me and whose arms comforted me, I would not have succeeded. The island was, of course, of my own making. I decided, as I have said, that I didn't have a past – my life started on 15th March 1976. I absolutely refused to look back, and to look beyond 24th June would have been stupid. My home, when I was able to get there, was my bolthole. There, my lovely girl listened to my problems, held me when I was down, encouraged me when I lost heart and never asked anything of me, except to know that she was loved.

The learning curve was much steeper than I imagined. Physically, I was fine, although my body was frequently pushed to the limit and often beyond. I lost about 12 pounds in weight in the first four weeks, but steadied at about 10 stone and stayed at that weight for the duration of my training and for about six months afterwards. My problems came with the very high academic requirements and public speaking. I had struggled through the educational requirements to apply and I was just about good enough to be accepted – but not good enough to succeed. Also, if I wasn't careful, I quickly slipped back into a strong, cockney accent. I am not suggesting for one moment that there is anything wrong with cockney or any other accent. In fact, accents are far more interesting to listen to than the so-called 'plummy' voices of the upper classes. But there is a line to be drawn. Someone once said that, "If you are listening to the accent, you're not hearing what's being spoken!"

The written requirements for OCTU were also quite strict. Not only were you obliged to keep a diary highlighting the day's events, which was handed in weekly for assessment, but there was also at least one essay a week on a set subject. And last, but not least, you also had to learn how to write all of the various forms of written communication required by the Officer Corp! So, in short, that was my Everest! I'd already fallen foul of the Education Officer who, after the first week, had said that he was 'concerned' about my written communication. So, on top of everything else, I set myself new targets for written and oral communications, with the aid of several grammar books. I set myself the target of at least one hour a day, regardless of the day's content, and that often meant burning the candle into the early hours, to re-learn nouns, pronouns, verbs, adverbs, adjectives and so on. I also set myself the target of reading *The Times* every day from cover to cover – regardless of the content – pronouncing the words slowly, but precisely to myself.

Ann, bless her, was also borrowing books from the library for my use as frequently as possible. So, soon I became familiar with T.S. Elliot, Charles Dickens, Henry Fielding, Daniel Defoe, George Bernard Shaw and so many other bygone literary figures. Much to the amusement of my fellow cadets on 'D' Flight, I started to speak slower too – thinking through what I was saying. The great majority were very supportive – one or two thought differently, but it was never voiced.

All this extra work, of course, took its toll. I remember quite clearly breaking down one weekend when I felt that it was all becoming too much. But, as always, Ann was there to calm me, support me, wrap me in her arms and put me back on track. The immediate outcome of this effort was that I produced slightly shorter written pieces – which was criticised – but I used better phraseology and I had improved punctuation and my writing was altogether easier to read. What they didn't know was that the final piece had been written two or three times until I was satisfied with it. I also slowed down my speech for presentations. This then gave me the opportunity to enunciate my words and think through sentence construction. All of my speeches, which included three 15-minute presentations, were all written in bold print, highlighting particular words, with coloured pencils being used to remind me when to enunciate, when to pause and huge black print reminders to make sure I did not drop certain letters – 'H' for example! The worst criticism I had, and one that I happily accepted, was that my speeches were laboured, "like walking through a sea of mud with swim fins on!" – to quote the Education Officer. The final assessment for my written and oral work was a C+ for which the Education Officer took full credit!

On the other hand however, I scored very high in terms of leadership qualities. My time at OCTU is best summed up by the closing comments of a speech made by the Commanding Officer of the American Officer Training Facility at Westpoint: "We take in a raw product, return it to putty, and then rebuild it into a leader of men!" Well, that's as may be, but what I also know is that I underwent a dramatic change in all aspects of my life – my vision, my attitudes, my ambitions! In every facet of my being, I changed. I wanted to be an officer – at times I wanted it more than breath. I had outgrown the alternatives! However, my Everest still remains! Regardless of what I have done or what I have accomplished, the goals that I set for my written and oral ambitions will always elude me!

However, the 24th June 1976 is a day I shall never forget. The passing out parade was spectacular. Hours and hours of drilling had trained a rather motley bunch into a precision-drilled squadron almost good enough to be part of the Queen's Colour Squadron. Well, we thought so! Amongst the hundreds of spectators, I actually managed to spot Ann, the boys and, best of all, my mother. They all waved, but what I remember most was the look of pride on my mother's face. I felt that, just maybe, I had balanced the scales, having broken her heart when I decided to give up dancing in 1956 and joined the RAF. I certainly hoped so. My step-father, Freddy, was there, but out of sight – he wasn't very good with crowds of people. The day was so memorable, especially when they removed our checkered hat bands – the last item that identified us as cadets and we were now officers!

During the reception, the Squadron Education Officer made his way over to our group and, for several seconds, he just stood looking at me with a huge smile on his face.

"Congratulations, David," he said, shaking my hand. "There were times when I very much doubted that you would succeed."

But, as he looked, smiling at my family, my beloved Ann and, in particular, my two mentors, he said, "I think I was probably the only one. I can't think of anybody who deserves this day more than you. I am overjoyed to be so wrong!"

I felt quite choked, but I managed to say, "Thank you."

To top it off, almost in unison, my mentors both said, "You obviously don't know him as well as we do!"

I was posted to RAF (Hospital) Ely in Cambridgeshire on 1st July 1976 as Flying Officer D. P. Dean.

CHAPTER 9

RAF (HOSPITAL) ELY

No matter how much training you do or how much you are brainwashed or, indeed, how much remodelling of you takes place – a thin ribbon on your shoulder feels 10 times the weight of three stripes and a crown. It required all of my self-assurance and confidence to arrive at RAF (H) Ely as an officer. I was definitely out of my comfort zone. Nevertheless, there was no turning back – I was no longer a Flight Sergeant. My arrival was helped considerably by the OC Admin. Squadron, who had also crossed over from the rank and file. He quickly put me at my ease and gave me a piece of advice that stayed with me for many years. "Use your years of experience, but think the problem through as an officer, not as an NCO: you will take on the mantle of an officer much quicker!" And with that sound advice he gave me three secondary duties!

So, as well as running a Catering Flight, which included a hospital, I also became the Liaison Officer for the local RAF Cadet Force, the officer responsible for Station and Hospital Broadcasting and the Liaison Officer for Family and Community Welfare. In short, if any serviceman or family had a welfare problem connected to the service, it came through me! For the first six months, my feet never touched the ground and, at times, it seemed that the mantle would never fit. But, slowly, with Ann always there to encourage me and often advise me, I suddenly felt comfortable in my new skin and with it came a new-found confidence. I enjoyed the recognition of my rank – by that, I mean I held the Queen's Commission and that was recognised by a salute, which I returned, from all non-commissioned personnel. I enjoyed being an officer. I enjoyed the responsibility and all that brought with it. I had ceased to think like an NCO. I always felt that Ely was a proving ground and in many ways it was. Whether it was just mixing with my brother officers, attending functions, formal or otherwise, or even being asked advice as the Officer in charge of that Flight. In all respects, I took every advantage to hone my skills. In November 1977, I was promoted to Flight Lieutenant and posted to RAF Brawdy in South Wales.

CHAPTER 10
RAF BRAWDY

I had always believed, like so many other re-treads before me, that Flight Lieutenant would be the summit of my career expectations. Very few Branch Officers expect to ever become a Squadron Leader. That's not a criticism of the system. Branch Officers definitely have a role, but age usually gets in the way of progressing further. Not that I was concerned about that when I was posted to Brawdy. But, because I had been promoted – as I thought, quite early – it was feasible that I could spend the next 18 years as a Flight Lieutenant! As I said though, it wasn't foremost in my mind when I arrived at Brawdy, as, for me, it was a really exciting Unit.

Since my return from Cyprus in 1971, all of my postings had been to Training or Headquarter Units, but Brawdy not only had aeroplanes, namely Hawker Hunter and its successor the BAE Hawk, but it was also home to a Search & Rescue Helicopter Squadron – initially, they used Whirlwinds but, a little later, the much-loved Sea Kings. During the early 1970s, which included my time at Brawdy, a low level tactical strike role was being developed. Previously, pilots had flown high-level operations in aircraft, such as the Avro Vulcan. Now they needed to be trained in low-level attack methods in aircraft like the Buccaneer and the new Jaguar. To achieve this at the Operational Conversion Units meant using highly expensive operational aircraft, which were badly needed elsewhere. Consequently, a Tactical Weapons Unit (TWU) was formed at RAF Brawdy specifically to teach these new skills. By the time I arrived in 1977, the Hunter was being replaced by a new jet trainer, the Hawk, which would be the basis of jet training into the 1980s. Now, if that isn't enough to get a newly promoted Flight Lieutenant excited, I don't know what is!

Just outside the main gate of Brawdy was an independent US Naval Base. Its role, as I have since found out courtesy of the Freedom of Information Act, was as an oceanographic research station used to track the movements of Russian submarines in the North Atlantic. History now records that RAF Brawdy was believed to be a priority target in the event of nuclear war with the Soviet Union! I'm glad I didn't know that in 1977. What I did find out was that all of the American personnel were on my station strength and were being fed in the respective messes, but those dining in the Junior Ranks' Mess were close to mutiny! More of that later.

In any event, between squadrons of jet aircraft, a Search & Rescue Helicopter Squadron and a large American Unit to cater for, together with a catering responsibility for the Marine Craft Unit at Tenby and the low level bombing range at Pembrey, there was a real buzz about the station. And, although I was slightly apprehensive about the size of my responsibilities, this fear was quickly diluted by the excitement I felt.

Another huge plus was that there were plenty of available married quarters, most of which were on estates in Haverfordwest which was near to the Unit, but the house on offer at Pembroke won hands down. Although a little further away across a causeway and situated between Pembroke and Pembroke Dock, it was located in a little estate called Buttermilk. A white, four-bedroomed 1920s style house, it was close to the shops, i.e. Pembroke Dock and the children's school. For me, it was about a 30 to 40 minute commute, but it was a beautiful house. The only complaint of any substance that I heard whilst we were living there was that learning the Welsh language, which was part of the children's school curriculum, was difficult. Ho hum!

On a social front, Ann had come into her own. She just took naturally to the officer's wife role. She regularly entertained her fellow wives at home and there were about 20 service couples and families in Buttermilk Close and it didn't take long to form friendships. She was either entertaining at home or being invited to someone else's home or a group of them would go off shopping. Always a beautiful woman, Ann now had a self-assurance about her that I hadn't recognised before. She took lessons and passed her driving test first time, and it only took her three months from making a decision to learn, to passing her test! We bought an Austin Mini for her, which she loved. It also gave her a little more independence.

It took me a little while to settle into my new post, mainly because of its diversity. The Officers' and Sergeants' Messes were running fine, as the staff in those messes were excellent and had manoeuvred skilfully around the Anglo-American feeding problems. Not so, I'm afraid, in the Junior Ranks' Mess. There, rather unfortunately, the mess was run with an iron fist by the Warrant Officer in charge who believed that, "When in Rome ... and so on," which is all very well if you want to close your eyes to the problem. Certainly, my investigations highlighted that the Warrant Officer had said to some of the Americans who had complained that, "This is England and if you don't like the food, don't eat it!" Actually, he was wrong from the outset – it was Wales! Although there was no paperwork to confirm or deny this action, one can only assume that my predecessor must have agreed with the Warrant Officer. In any event, I decided that firstly, I would, with the help of the American Commanding Officer, Captain Arni Laux, talk to the disgruntled troops. Fortunately for me, Captain Laux was first and foremost a gentleman but, like me, had only been in post six weeks and had only just recently been informed of the problem. So, my arrival at the US Base pre-empted a request from him.

From that point onwards, we saw quite a lot of each other and became firm friends. A forum was set up in one of the large assembly halls for me to meet and discuss the problem with the junior ranks. With hindsight, without the Captain and two other officers present, I'm not sure I would have been safe! Even with them there, it was touch and go for the first 10 minutes. There were about 60 in the audience, all junior ranks. After listening to them for a while, I thought that their main concerns were simple and would require very little from my stall to quell the riot!

Their main concerns were breakfast and puddings. For breakfast, they couldn't understand why waffles weren't available, and why couldn't the likes of pumpkin pie be made available occasionally? Thinking on my feet, I told them that I would discuss the problem through with the various agencies, but that in one week, I would put the matter right – I hoped! There were some other issues, mainly the way they were treated by the staff when they made requests, but I believed that the fundamental problem was the issue of their diet. There were lots of grunts and groans, like, "Yeah, we've heard all that before!" or "Talk is cheap!" and "C'mon, he's no different from the guy before him!" But I was! An hour later, I had arranged, or Captain Laux had arranged, to have three double waffle griddles delivered to the mess from which the troops could make their own waffles! Through a local purchase order from my office to the American PX, I arranged to purchase the mix for waffle batter, which just required milk, plus maple syrup and some banana mix which was also enjoyed at breakfast, and the mix for sweet potato pie, pumpkin pie and others. All I had to do now was discuss it with the Warrant Officer! Unfortunately, it became a bit of a one-sided conversation. The Warrant Officer accused me of being too soft and that the 'Yanks' were taking advantage of me. Oh, and that he knew best because he was the Warrant Officer and that he thought that I was sticking my nose into an area that didn't concern me! It did actually get a little worse – he threatened to resign if I undermined his authority. One hour later though, he had agreed, following my suggestion that the night shift would prepare the batter for the waffles ready with the necessary syrups for self-use by whoever wanted them in the morning. Thus, by using the various fillings issued from the PX, a variety of American-type sweets would be made available on a regular basis, but not less than four times a week. We quickly established a standard order to the PX and they delivered once a week. The problem of unhappy Americans disappeared and the Warrant Officer? Well, he left the service one year later. I've always been grateful for his support in the implementation of a new challenge!

At the next Airmen's Mess committee meeting, which the Catering Officer chairs – a committee which is designed so that the junior ranks can air their grievances – two items were noted. One of the members on the committee was now an American sailor and, secondly, that the British troops also thought the idea of waffles for breakfast was a brilliant idea!

It was an incredibly active Unit and, as my mind flicks back, I realise I could probably write a small book just about Bawdy. I actually issued 'rum' twice during my two winters – an old custom which was still in vogue in the late 1970s when personnel were required to work outdoors in inclement weather for long periods. The winters in Wales are brutal! It was also the first time that I met Prince Charles. He visited Brawdy a couple of times a year, primarily to fly the Hawk – but luncheon had to be arranged. I remember he was particularly fond of steak and kidney pudding!

My final memory of Brawdy is a bad one though – which also brought back bad memories from an earlier time. There had been a spate of thefts in the Officers' Mess, apparently going back to before my arrival, but they had escalated during my time. The thefts were mainly of alcohol and cigarettes from the bar stock. They had been investigated quite fully by the officer in charge of the police, but their findings were inconclusive, so they called in the military CID. In my own experience, if you fall under their radar – and the Catering Officer does – they just ride roughshod over you. It was shortly after that I faced a particularly awful grilling – their attitude was that theft within the perimeters of my responsibility must, by definition, involve the Catering Officer! I had written several statements and, although innocent, felt frightened and, justifiably so.

The reason for my worries about the thefts was that as a younger man, I'd had a scary brush with the law. In the late autumn of 1959, having been married only two or three months, Ann and I were invited to a party some distance from where we lived. We were being ferried to and from the party by a mutual friend who owned a car and, indeed, we were staying overnight in his married quarters at RAF Denbury. On the return journey, he crammed about eight of us in his car with me and another in the front with the driver and Ann with the remaining four on top of one another in the back. It was late and we were all tipsy and very happy, laughing all the way back to Denbury. When Ann and I finally got out of the car at our chum's house, she seemed upset. I asked her what was wrong and, although she had clearly been crying, she insisted she was alright. I took her arm, stopped her and told her she wasn't alright and that we weren't going anywhere until she told me the truth. It turned out that one of the fellows on the back seat had tried to stick his hand up her shirt and, although she stopped him, it really upset her.

Well, I was almost manic with rage. My chum told me where he lived and, although all three told me not to, I hammered on the door until it was opened by his wife, and told her I wanted to speak to her husband. To cut a long story short, because I was making so much noise, he finally came downstairs. He said he was sorry in response to my accusation and said it was just the drink. I smacked him in the face anyway and told him to apologise to Ann, which he did. I also told him that if he came within 50 yards of me or Ann ever again, I would kill him!

I now wind forward to the spring of 1960. I was barbequing a pig for the church on the green in Denbury village as part of the village fête. At some point, I looked up and who should be walking towards me, unaware that it was me, but the arse who had assaulted Ann. I picked up a rod of iron which was used to help turn the pig on the spit and shouted to the arse that if he came any closer I would cleave his bloody head in. He quickly realised who it was and turned tail. So there I am, waving my rod of iron and screaming at the top of my voice, "If you come near my wife again, you bastard, I'll kill you!"

Later on in that year, following a bad accident on my motorbike, I bought a black 1938 Morris Series E car. It was a lovely motor, but it did require quite a bit of repair work to the body. So one weekend in September, I decided to repair the front nearside wing which was pretty well riddled with rust. It wasn't a bad job, but it quite obviously hadn't been repaired by a professional. About two months later, having just completed a week of late shifts in the Airmen's Mess, I was hauled in for questioning by the CID in regard to the death of an airman who was apparently walking along the same road that I used to go home. The airman was hit in the back by a passing car and thrown into a ditch where he died. They managed to ascertain that it was a black car and that it would clearly have damage to the front nearside wing and that his time of death was between 20-22.00 hrs. In fact, it was just about the time that I would be on my way home from work! Added to which, I had recently repaired the nearside wing on my black car, and the body in the ditch was none other than the same person who had assaulted Ann and who I had been overheard threatening to kill.

The next three and half months were hell. I was under caution half of that time and held on the Unit. Friends looked after Ann, who was about six to seven months pregnant. At times, the interrogations were brutal and done so cleverly that I began to believe that I was actually guilty. However, by mid-December, the so-called evidence was still circumstantial and the farmer's wife whose property our caravan was parked on came forward to say that she had seen me repairing the nearside wing much earlier than the accident and, not after, which the CID took into account. Nevertheless, they still believed that I was guilty, but their evidence never got better than circumstantial. However, in my favour, responding to an advert which had been placed in the village for any witnesses to the accident, a lady had come forward to say that she had seen a black car speeding away from the village at about 19.45 – a time for which I had an alibi. I'm not sure that any of this altered their opinion – but it was just an opinion and something that they just couldn't prove. Incidentally, I met the officer in charge of the investigation again in 1970 and, although he raised the subject with a smile, he said that he had never changed his opinion about my guilt. Ho hum!

Nonetheless, these experiences meant I had a dislike of police investigations, for obvious reasons! In due course, it turned out that the culprit behind the thefts in the Officers' Mess at RAF Brawdy, turned out to be Sergeant Stewart. It was felt, however, that I should carry a certain amount of the responsibility as he was a member of my Flight and that better checks should have been in place. I suppose one could say that my tour at Brawdy ended on a low note, but it was not, however, reflected in my annual report. So, by November 1979, I was on my way to RAF Hereford.

CHAPTER 11

RAF HEREFORD

This Unit and tour turned out to be pivotal in my life to come. Everything that I did always returned to Hereford: it was the source of my self-examination. Although I was posted to RAF Hereford, I was, in fact, posted to the RAF School of Catering as a Flight Commander. The School of Catering was a small Unit in its own right, attached to RAF Hereford. It was also closing down! The school was moving to pastures new. The new posting was to be RAF Aldershot, and although the move wasn't finished until 1985, the effects were being felt already. There were fewer courses and that awful feeling of everything being run-down. It is probably a weakness in me, but I never felt completely committed.

The other initial problem was that there was a waiting list for married quarters. Therefore, I was separated from the family for some time. Tony, my eldest son, had applied and been accepted for Royal Marine Commando training in October 1978, so Ann just had the two younger boys at home. Colin, the second eldest, was considering following me into the Air Force – he would be 17 in the December. Andrew, the youngest, and by far the more studious, was still immersed in learning.

My responsibilities in the school were for all the cooking aspects of the courses, whereas my opposite number was responsible for all the stewarding. We were also jointly responsible for the training of all young officers who had applied to become Catering Officers. Yes, it was the same course that I had completed both as a Flight Sergeant and as a Flying Officer. Other than us, there was a Warrant Officer who was responsible for training in the office side of the business, but I believe he also came under my opposite number – we were nothing without our chain of command. And, above us all, was a Squadron Leader who, of course, we all deferred to. Although I enjoyed the work, it didn't seem to stretch me. I'm not sure whether it was the thought that the school was moving on or whether there were just too few challenges! I know my opposite number never felt like that because he was forever rewriting steward courses or coming up with innovative ideas that would improve the training, whereas I just did enough so that the Flight ticked over!

You know what they say – the devil makes work for idle hands. A part of my job was to organise trips out for the junior officers to visit various stations or organisations to help with their learning process – this is what it was like at the sharp end! It was during one of those trips that I ended up in bed with one of the trainee catering officers. I would like to make excuses for my behaviour, but there aren't any. For whatever reason, the old Dixie Dean had re-emerged. Even as I write this, I hate myself all over again. How could I possibly do this to Ann? The woman who was always beside me, who had supported me and loved me regardless, and who was the mother of my children? It's unthinkable – but it happened. The relationship didn't last long, but the effects are still with me today. Guilt!

Some short time later, after we had moved into a married quarter and the woman in question had moved on to her first posting, the guilt of what I had done was slowly eating away at my soul and was noticeable in my weight loss. One day, returning from a visit to my parents who lived in Ramsgate, together with Ann's brother and wife who were in their own car behind us, I suddenly blurted out, "I need you to divorce me!"

"What?" Ann said. "You want a divorce? Why?"

And it all came tumbling out. *I had an affair, it's all over now but I can't live with the guilt* and so on. I'm sure you've heard such stories before. I said I was sorry, and I was, but it sounded so hollow and hardly sufficient considering the pain I was causing her.

"Do you love her?" she asked, now crying bitterly.

"I thought I did, at the time," I said, "but, no I don't love her and I don't think I ever did!" Tears were now streaming down my face. "I am so sorry," I repeated.

"Stop the car! Stop the car!" Ann said.

I pulled into a lay-by, followed by her brother. We both got out of the car, but Ann just walked up to her brother's car, opened the rear door and got in beside our youngest son, Andrew, who had wanted to travel with his aunty and uncle. I just stood there. Their car drove by me with my brother and sister-in-law registering their feelings with stares of hate. Andrew, I could see, was crying and holding onto his mother, whose head was bowed. I just stood there, tears streaming down my face, wondering how on earth I had managed to throw so much away.

I sat in the car for I don't know how long when I had this overwhelming need to get to a church. Knowing that I wouldn't find a church on the arterial road, I took the first turning off and just drove. I turned many times and had no idea where I was when suddenly I arrived outside a church – and although I had tried several times over the years, I was never able to find this church again. I entered through a large creaking gothic doorway into the gloom, which I have come to believe is reminiscent of old churches. I didn't look to see if anybody else was there – I just made my way to the first pew, which was accessed by a little gate. Thinking back, if other people had been there and they were kneeling, I wouldn't have seen them anyway – and the pew sides were so high that even if you were sitting, you could only see heads! All of this was only apparent in hindsight though. But I did realise now that as I knelt down I could neither see nor be seen.

Almost outside of my control, I cried out to the Lord. "Help me! Please help me!" I confessed aloud all that I had done and that I was truly repentant and begged for the opportunity to put things right. I think I knelt there for an absolute age – I don't really know how long it was – but suddenly, I started to get warm, almost as though someone had turned the heating on which was unlikely, as it was late summer. Even so, it became almost oppressive, almost unbearable. My head started to swim and I thought I was going to lose consciousness! Then, suddenly, I felt a voice. I know that sounds bizarre – but I didn't 'hear' a voice, I 'felt' it – and the message was clear. If I was a sceptic, I would say that it was my subconscious telling me to do what was in my heart – and that was to prostrate myself before Ann and beg her forgiveness. But I'm not a sceptic – so I now felt that the Lord was an ally.

I drove as fast as I could, but I still didn't arrive home until dark. It was then that I realised that I must have been in the church for hours! To cut a long story short, Ann did forgive me and I promised never to stray again – a promise that is still good today, 35 years later. However, I have never been able to forgive myself. I tried so hard to immerse myself in work, but there just wasn't the challenging work that I needed, to be done. And, clearly, I lacked the interest. Of course, things were still difficult at home – and it was no fault of Ann's. The guilt was pouring out of me and I felt that I was constantly walking on eggshells. I was so frightened of doing or saying something wrong that I was overly polite and contrite, and if it had not been for the intervention of my Squadron Leader, who was obviously quite astute and who realised that something was wrong, I might even have destroyed my second chance with Ann. Although Ann was faultless, I now believe that she thought that my quietness and politeness was because I missed the other woman – which wasn't true.

One evening in early January 1980, the Squadron Leader (for the purposes of this book we will call him Mike) knocked on the door of our married quarters and suggested that, along with him, Ann and I commence training with a view to gaining team places for the Wye to Chepstow raft race which was to take place in the forthcoming May. We were both excited about this idea, although I believe for different reasons. Mike went on to say that if I was successful in gaining a place on the team, Ann, plus his wife, Sally, and some of the others would be required to form a support team. At last, I had something to get a grip on – a challenge I so desperately needed. And we both had something else to think about.

The training was gruelling – we went to the gym three or four times a week for strength and fitness training, with a run beforehand starting at three miles, but by April becoming 10 miles. Ann and Sally assumed straightaway that we would be selected, so started to plan the accommodation, which were to be tents in a nearby field, with food, liquids and a route that they could travel to in order to give us support from the sidelines. It took over our lives. As a result, Ann and myself gradually grew closer and the past slowly receded. By the April of that year, I felt we were almost back to normal. But my behaviour must have left some sort of blemish on our relationship because Ann, as I came to believe, now had a deep-rooted mistrust of me, which, to be fair, rarely surfaced – but I felt it was there. And, in me, there was and still is a dormant guilt that never quite goes away, but this was a small, though totally regrettable penalty for me to pay to have my lovely girl back.

We did get selected for the team and though we only came 43rd out of 50 teams, I wouldn't have missed it for the world. Mike and I became firm friends, but he never once broached the subject of why he'd asked me to train for the team. Such a friend!

By June that year, my boredom had started to return though. The workload at the school had continued to decrease and, unlike my opposite number on the steward side, I was unable to be creative – and the restlessness started once again. And yet, once again, although Mike never said it, I believe it was he who recommended me to take over as the Officer Commanding the RAF Regiment Flight in the absence of the Regiment Officer who had been called away. I was absolutely made up – this was a world that I loved! I got on well with the staff and very quickly was joining them on their training exercises in the field – I was so grateful I'd done the training for the raft team! I even began to rewrite some of the training exercises and input some of my own ideas. I was with them for four months – four months of hard work, weariness and challenge and I couldn't have been happier.

That September, I was asked to report to the Station Commander who informed me that I had been recommended to take over as the Officer's Club Manager at NATO HQ in Brunssum, Holland (AFCENT). I was told to visit the Unit, in particular, the Officers' Club, and advise the MOD if I was prepared to take over the post! I could never remember a time when I was asked to go somewhere and I was fairly sure that the reason for the request would become clear.

I did, indeed, visit and although I was certain that it would be a challenging post, I, nevertheless, agreed. Ann, despite everything we'd been through, supported me wholeheartedly. Having found a good boarding school (Bedstone College) for Andrew to finish his education prior to university, Ann and I left for Holland at the end of October 1981. By now, Colin, our second son, had also joined the RAF and followed me into the catering branch as a cook.

CHAPTER 12

AFCENT

A little bit of background on this Unit might be useful. AFCENT (Air Force Central Europe) is one of three NATO Headquarters throughout Europe. The other two are AFSOUTH (based in Naples) and AFNORTH (based in Norway). Because all the units are international i.e. NATO and from one the largest nations within the treaty (America) it has, over the years, fallen to them to create the strategy for catering and social affairs. In essence, instead of a Sergeants' Mess and an Officers' Mess which you would expect to find on any Royal Air Force Unit, AFCENT has an 'All Ranks Club' with a separate dining facility which, at AFCENT, was jointly run between an RAF Warrant Officer and the equivalent in American rank, and an NCO Club which provides all the dining and entertainment and is run by an American Club Manager who is usually a Chief Master Sergeant (a sort of super-duper Warrant Officer). There is also an Officers' Club which also runs on the American club system and which also provides the dining, bar and entertainment facilities for all officers. Also attached to the club at AFCENT was a 30-room hotel, mostly used for transiting officers, but, in my time, it did accommodate one 2 Star Canadian General, one 2 Star Dutch General and one Belgium Colonel. The manager of the club/hotel is usually filled on a rotational basis, i.e. any of the NATO members could be called upon to do their turn. The reality was that it usually fell between the Americans and the British. However, the management team in all of the clubs, where possible, was drawn from all members of NATO. The one main exception to this arrangement was that the manager of the NCO Club, purely because of its complexity, was always held by an American, usually a Chief Master Sergeant.

For example, when I arrived at AFCENT, the top post in the Officers' Club was held by a British Flight Lieutenant, supported by one American Chief Master Sergeant, with all the other main departments overseen by NCOs drawn from the other NATO members. The dining room, bar and stewarding were managed by a Dutch Warrant Officer. The accounts and office were overlooked by a Belgium Warrant Officer and the kitchen was overseen by a British Sergeant chef. All of these departments were supported by British, Dutch, Belgium, American and French NCOs. The remainder of the staff, which numbered about 40, were mostly Dutch civilians.

My appointment to the post was a little unusual and not without its problems. The British staff were only halfway through their tours of duty as Officers' Club Managers when the British Officer in post at the time was fired and returned to the UK for being a naughty boy (you don't need to know any more). So during a period of three to four months between his departure and my arrival, the club had been run by his deputy, an American Chief Master Sergeant and, frankly, he didn't want to relinquish the reins! His name was Fred Pettus and he was an extremely talented and capable NCO with about 25 years of club management experience behind him. I also found him to be overbearing and self-important. More of that later. Rather unfortunately for me, unlike all of my British predecessors, I did my club training at USAF Lakenheath in Suffolk, whereas my predecessors had completed their six weeks in America! Ho hum!

On our arrival, Ann and I spent our first night in Holland in 'my' hotel and the following day, we waited for our furniture and so on to arrive from UK, and then we moved into a three-bedroomed semi at 41 Franz Hallstraat, Brunssum. The next 10 days were so confusing, it was almost laughable. Besides all of the normal arrival procedures, I had so many people to meet. My immediate boss was a Wing Commander who, in turn, worked for an American Colonel who was in charge of an enormous 'wing,' consisting of the catering, the clubs, supplies, motor transport and all of the administration and accounts of those independent squadrons. His wing was called ASG (AFCENT Support Group). His weekly meetings with his team – which, rather unfortunately, included me – were held in his office at 07.00 hrs every Monday.

After my arrival, and rather to my surprise, I was ordered to attend a meeting with the Deputy Commander in Chief of AFCENT, Air Chief Marshal, Sir John Gingell, who, amongst his many other responsibilities, had taken a direct interest in the Officers' Club and in particular, the new manager – me! Because of the nature of my predecessor's departure, he wanted to make it perfectly clear to the new incumbent that he would not tolerate any indiscretions whatsoever. He felt that we, the Royal Air Force, had already embarrassed ourselves sufficiently in the eyes of our fellow NATO members and that it was time to prove that we could 'do the job' and wipe the smear away. He went on to say that he took the incident personally. When he had completed the 'browbeating,' through which I stood to attention, he then smiled and told me to remove my cap and sit down. He went on to say, in a much friendlier tone, that he knew that it would be an uphill job, but his door would always be open to me and that I didn't need to go through channels, but just inform his ADC and he would do whatever was needed to smooth my path. How's that for a friend? Okay, so maybe he wasn't a friend, but what an ally! I never did ask to see him though, but that didn't stop him from asking me if everything was okay when we crossed paths in the Officers' Club.

As if it couldn't get any better, Ann and I went to afternoon tea with him about four months later and we had a formal dinner together a few months before his return to the UK. Shortly after his return, I think it was about 1986/7, he was given the distinct honour of becoming Black Rod in Parliament until his retirement in 1992. It is with much sorrow that I must report that he passed away in 2009. Ann and I felt proud and privileged to have known such a gentleman.

A little more background on how the club worked may be useful. The club was run on purely commercial lines – a budget was set and the Club Manager was expected to achieve it! Unlike most businesses, however, it wasn't expected to make a huge profit. The budget was set by a Board of Governors who were influenced and advised by the Wing Commander of the ASG, my boss and myself. The Board of Governors was 'made up' of one senior officer from every NATO country at AFCENT. The budget, when I arrived, was set at one and a half million guilders (about £300,000) – the guilder being the Dutch currency at the time. About one third of this amount was gathered through members' subscriptions, and the remainder was the main task of the Club Manager to accrue. During my time at AFCENT, I achieved this by making the Officers' Club the 'place to be' for food, entertainment, drink, functions (private or otherwise) and I also sold the space to businesses for their events! The Officers' Club was the place to be if you were a company selling jewellery, gold, diamonds, artwork, china – almost anything you can think of – and I took 10% of their sales in commission, for the club. I would sell anything if it was legal and if I thought there was a market. I even sold a 'Haggis Hunt' to 28 Americans, for which I had to apologise afterwards by giving them half price tickets to the first Burns Night! In essence, that was all the job was about – improving standards in both the hotel and club and making it the most popular place in town! I even ran a casino, made up of 30 gaming machines, from which the club took a large percentage of its profits – and they still paid out 60% to the punter. The club regularly made 100,000 guilders per annum!

Of all my achievements at the club, the one that I am probably the most proud of is my specialist dining room. We had three restaurants: one for daily luncheons and large evening functions, a smaller one for formal luncheons or dinners, and my 'piece de resistance' was a dining room I created called the 'Alliance Rooms'. It was open Thursday to Saturday evenings and seated up to 40 covers and had to be pre-booked. To the soft notes of a baby grand piano, you would be served with the likes of lobster thermidor, chateaubriand steak carved at your table, and flambéed fruit. For the last two and half years of my four-year tour, there was rarely a night when it wasn't full. It was not only 'top drawer', but a great money maker too. As I had the power to appoint or sack any or all civilian staff, I was, at times, ruthless. My aim was always to achieve the highest possible standards in all departments. If, after two warnings, the individual concerned was falling short of my ideal, I just fired him or her and then rehired. During my time at AFCENT, I replaced one accountant, two chefs, four barmen, six stewards, five general cleaners and one storeman. When I left, I honestly believed that, under the guidance of the heads of departments, the club could run itself – the staff were that good. I remember saying much earlier in the book that each tour had one or two events that made it memorable. That wasn't the case at AFCENT – it was more like 15-20! I will select just a few though, to 'whet' your appetite.

The first three to four months of my tour were sheer hell. Even with the benefit of my weeks of training at USAF Lakenheath, the learning curve was steep. There was so much to take in and it was all made more difficult because I seriously believed that Chief Master Sergeant Pettus was working against me – it wasn't difficult to make me look foolish and he took every opportunity to do so. Every night, if I wasn't in the club, Ann and I would walk and talk, hoping to find solutions to various problems, many of which I believed started with Pettus.

At my lowest ebb one evening during our walk, Ann just said, "Could you manage without him?"

I looked at her for a minute or two, trying to collect my thoughts and said, "Yes – it would initially be difficult, but yes, I could manage!"

"Good," she said. "So, get rid of him!"

I looked at her. I couldn't believe what she said.

"Get rid of him." she repeated. "Look, if he's holding you back and clearly working against you, go and see his superior officer in the American Delegation and ask them to find him another job."

You know, she was absolutely right. I could have whooped for joy. Instead, I gave her a great big kiss and, for the first time, I felt confident in my role.

The next morning, I made an appointment to see the Personnel Officer at the American Delegation – a Major Arni Briggs. I explained the problem to him, but as I was doing so, it did cross my mind that he was a fellow American, so why should he support me? But guess what? He did!

"Look," he said. "I know Pettus – he's an incredibly talented man but he can also be an arse. So, go back and tell him that he's no longer needed in the club and that he's to report to me for reassignment. He won't believe you, so just tell him that he's fired and that you no longer need him."

With some trepidation, I called Pettus into my office and, in his usual manner, he went to sit down in the chair opposite.

"Stand up, Chief," I said. "You're not going to be here long enough to get comfortable." I went on to say that his services were no longer required in the Officer's Club and that he was to report to Major Briggs for reassignment. His face said, 'You're joking!' So, rather dismissively,

I just said, "You can leave now, Chief and, truthfully, I hope that I never see you again."

Well, his jaw was just opening and closing with no sound coming out. He finally said, "You can't do that. You can't fire me! You'll never manage without me!"

I looked him straight in the eyes and said, "No, Chief. I can't manage *with* you. You are not part of my team. You still believe that you run this club – well, guess what? You don't, I do! Now get out! And shut the door behind you."

And he did. I sat down in my chair and you know what? I was shaking. But, for the first time in four months, I felt in control. Major Briggs phoned me about an hour later and said that, initially, he put Pettus on leave for a few weeks and that he would return to his office for reassignment. He went on to ask that if Pettus was prepared to be part of my team, would I take him back? I said that I would think about it, but it would be dependent on Pettus accepting me as the Club Manager and that his only role was to support me. If there was just one incident where he made a decision without consulting me, he would be back on leave again, but this time indefinitely.

It took him six weeks, but he finally rang my secretary to ask if he could make an appointment to see me. He didn't try to sit down when he came in and I left him standing on purpose. It was the most contrite I have ever seen him and I believed that he wanted to start over. All of this was done with his eyes pointing downwards. I left him like that for about 10 seconds and then I put out my hand and said, "Welcome back, Fred. Let's talk about the future." Fred became a brilliant 'wing man' and a good friend. He also taught me to play racket ball.

Whilst this had been going on, Ann was also being interviewed for a job as an assistant accountant in the NCO Club. With hindsight, her success at achieving the position became, for me, a double-edged sword. I strongly believe that the stress of this job played a part in our early retirement from the Royal Air Force in 1987. Although I wasn't aware of it at the time, she became responsible for the day-to-day entries in separate ledger accounts for every NATO country! This was, of course, pre-Euro and pre-computer accounts, so she kept separate ledger accounts for American dollars, Dutch guilders, English pounds, French francs and so on. The job was an absolute nightmare – and yet I never heard one complaint from her. In fact, over and above her work, she also attended every function that required my attendance and that could be as little as twice a week or as much as four times a week. Again, there was never a complaint. She was an absolute natural at playing first lady – with her confidence and good looks, I'm sure she fluttered many a heart!

I thought I would recall a couple of tongue-in-cheek stories. The Commander in Chief of AFCENT until 1983 was a German 4 Star General, Von Senger und Etterlin – it's a bit of a mouthful. This gentleman was not a great lover of the British because, apparently, as a result of a skirmish with the said British during the

Second World War, he lost an arm and an eye! I almost understand this, but, anyway, the General avoided talking to the British – it was usually left to his ADC. However, during 1983, and shortly before he handed over to a General Chalupa, his German successor as C in C, we were obliged to host a visit from Queen Beatrix, the Queen of the Netherlands. Part of that visit was a formal luncheon in the Officers' Club, comprising the heads of the various delegations, plus a few hangers on! The total in number was 24. Van Senger was so worried about the success of this visit that I was ordered to his office to discuss the details. I was informed by his ADC prior to entering that I must smartly walk the 30 feet from door to desk, salute and remain at attention. He, the ADC, would then speak on behalf of his General, but I must be aware that his words were direct orders from the General. So, there I was. To be honest, if he'd had his hat on, I would have felt that I was being court marshalled! I was very uncomfortable.

The visit from Queen Beatrix was in six weeks' time. The ADC, reading from his notes, said, "The General would like a menu in three days' time, and the food is to be light and only three courses. There will be a rehearsal every Monday afternoon for the next four weeks, attended by all diners, of which he will attend the last one to ensure the smoothness of the event. All officers, with him as the exception, will be in the dining room, behind their respective chairs, leaving sufficient room for the Queen to enter and walk in front of them

– she does not walk behind the backs of people – and the General will guide her to her seat. The General will sit beside her, and, when she is seated, the assembled company can do likewise. Only at that point will the staff enter with the first course."

During all this, his one good eye never blinked and never left my face. "The General also wants you to be fully aware of the importance of this visit, particularly for him, and anything less than perfection will be unacceptable."

With the good eye still unwavering, I was informed that I could now leave, but that I must return in three days with my suggested menu. It's worth mentioning at this point that the dining rooms and kitchen, aside from the military presence, were run by two of the finest caterers I have ever had the pleasure to work with. The Maître d' was Hinnie Bertram, an absolute master at his job, and the kitchen was run by a Chef de cuisine, Jos Ploum, an exceptional chef. Both were involved in the Sittard and Heerlen Hotel Colleges and were held in very high regard for their expertise, and both had been in post at the Officers' Club for a couple of decades. So, with my background, as you'll remember, leading the Royal team from 1974 until getting my commission – what was a little old luncheon for a Queen? I will spare you the details. Suffice to say, it all went splendidly. So much so that Queen Beatrix signed a menu for me. And I'm probably wrong, but I thought I saw Von Senger smile! (I'm definitely wrong.)

About a year earlier, in September 1982, AFCENT had another important visitor – this time from SHAPE (Supreme HQ Allied Powers Europe), in the form of General Haig. Although a luncheon was booked for him and other military heads at NATO, we had been asked to host a seminar of clerical heads, which had been booked for some time. Although security was paramount for Haig, it was felt that a couple of dozen vicars, who would be subject to being searched anyway, wouldn't pose a threat. General Haig and the vicars arrived, as arranged, about 15 minutes apart, the vicars arriving first with their seminar and luncheon being held in the Alliance Rooms and General Haig being wined and dined in the Torwood Room, with a distance of some 40-50 yards between them.

Suddenly, the alarm was sounded by one of the security guards because he had found a briefcase secreted under an armchair in the foyer. Well, all hell was let loose! Everybody had to leave the building and the bomb squad was called in. Amidst all this confusion, one of the vicars was trying to say something to one of the security team, but to no avail as their brief was clear – everybody out! The bomb squad finally agreed that the offending case was not dangerous, but this didn't prevent them from removing it to a safe area for destruction! Having destroyed it and its contents, they then found out from the vicar that it held his vestment! Ho hum!

Here's a quick story that always brings a sad smile to my face. Like most Units in the UK, the Officers' Clubs had respective Wives' Clubs, formed of course, from the various delegations. These clubs were very busy and in some ways, tried to outdo each other in size and the variation and grandeur of their respective functions. I knew most of the wives in the British Wives' Club and some, indeed most, were very nice, even though they could be demanding at times, as only women can be! You know, right room, right décor, right menu, right cutlery and so on – but they were always very nice about it. Except one, and this was Mrs Crowhurst. She was always impeccably turned out – the nails matched the hair, the hair matched the shoes, the shoes matched the clothes and all of this matched the handbag. She must have spent hours on her appearance! Mind you, like most of the woman at AFCENT, she had little else to do, but to go for coffee with her neighbours. She was also pretentious, loud, domineering and acutely aware of her husband's rank. He was a Wing Commander, although the way she spoke to the other wives and the club staff, including me, you would have thought he was an Air Vice Marshall! She was a thoroughly disagreeable person. In 1982, she had nominated herself to organise a joint Wives' Club Fête to be held at Gutersloh – an RAF Station just over the border in Germany. This event was to be similar to a village fête, but on a much grander scale. All the Wives' Clubs, including Gutersloh, numbering about 12, were each to organise a fundraising event with all the monies going to charity. Gutersloh had granted a piece of land where the respective marquees were to be raised.

I had endured weeks of tantrums, demands for glassware, plateware, cutlery, tables, tablecloths – Mrs. Crowhurst's list was endless, as was her finger-jabbing, her orders, her demands on the time of my staff and her constant threats that her husband, the Wing Commander, would hear about anything and everything that didn't go her way.

This culminated in her demanding my attendance at Gutersloh with the Wives' Club to help organise the marquee layout on paper for the whole fête. I tried everything to avoid this unnecessary visit, but she finally enlisted the help of her husband, so I reluctantly went along. She had organised a bus to take all of the wives and myself to the allocated site. When we arrived, I pointed out to Mrs. Crowhurst that, due to its proximity to the runway, the area was very exposed to all weathers – not least a vicious crosswind. As usual, she just said that I was being negative and, as the club wasn't making money out of the venture, I was being obstructive. Regardless of the wind, she ordered everybody off the bus so that she could better illustrate where she thought the marquees should be. Just as I was thinking through how difficult it would be to construct a marquee village in such high winds, a cry went up. Everybody turned their eyes as a long-haired creature scampered as fast as the wind could carry it towards the runway. The screaming continued, only now I realised that it was Mrs. Crowhurst.

"Get it! Get it, please!" she implored me, grabbing my arm. As I looked at her, I realised that it was her wig that was scampering towards the runway! Amidst the laughter of some of the wives, I did run after the wig – but only because Mrs Crowhurst was crying and totally bereft. She was trying desperately to cover what appeared to be a badly scarred scalp with her hands, which unfortunately didn't hide the fact that she had little or no hair!

Mrs Crowhurst changed overnight, and even with her wig firmly back in place, she was never quite so high and mighty again! The fête did happen, but on a smaller scale and it was held at AFCENT. In her defence though, it was a brilliant piece of organisation.

Whilst I realise that I could probably write a book just about my time at AFCENT, that is not the reason for writing this particular book, so I shall curtail my enthusiasm and include just a couple more shorter stories to conclude this chapter. Our youngest son, Andrew, did not quite achieve our desires for his education at Bedstone College, primarily due to his over-active loins! A remark made by his house tutor was that, "If Andrew spent as much time on his maths and English as he does on refining his skills in human biology, he would be a Grade 'A' student. Unfortunately, he cannot be graded for the number of times he's been caught in the girls' dorm – only chastised! Further education might well benefit him." To that end, we took him out of college in June 1982 and installed him in the Kent School near RAF Rheindalen. He was a partial boarder – Monday to Friday – but spent every weekend at home, which also meant that he spent an awful lot of time in the Officers' Club. Indeed, I employed him, part-time, in the stores department. Although I'm delighted to say he finally achieved the scholastic results required for him to enter the Royal Air Force, it did not curb his appetite, I'm given to understand, in honing his skills in human biology! He finally joined the RAF in September 1985 as an Electronics L. Tech. Airfields and gained a commission in 1992 as an F/O Air Traffic Controller.

Whilst we were serving at AFCENT, one of the most difficult periods for Ann and myself occurred, and as always, a shared crisis, brought us ever closer together. Tony, our eldest son, joined the Royal Marine Commandos during our tour at Ely in October 1977 after completing his training in September 1978. From Lympstone in Devon, where he completed his training, he was posted to the opposite end of the island to join the 45 Commandos in Arbroath, Scotland. During the next four and a half years, he did three tours in Norway and two in Northern Ireland and also managed to get married in December 1981. Alas, the marriage only lasted one year. In April of 1982, he was on board the Sir Tristram with 5,000 other troops en route to the Falkland Islands when war broke out between the UK and Argentina.

Like most service families, you only ever get the bare bones of tours and incidents, so the detail of both his Norwegian and Northern Ireland tours only came to light years later. Nevertheless, we were aware he was on board the Sir Tristram and, for my part, I was both excited and proud of his forthcoming adventure. Ann, of course, always worried about the boys, but nothing compared to the worry and anxiety when we heard that The Galahad had been blown up almost upon its arrival in the Falklands. We couldn't help thinking that other troop carriers could suffer the same fate. Most of the nation, including us, only received information on the war from media reports. Ann was so distressed because we knew that Tony was in the area and the media suggested that there were no survivors. We were beside ourselves with worry, so I decided to contact the Air Chief Marshall who, I was sure, had better intelligence than we did – and he did say 'his door was always open.' And, indeed, it was.

Returning my call, he informed us that Tony had been part of the forward party who had left his ship en route to Stanley. The relief was so overwhelming that we just hugged each other and cried, although we knew he was certainly not out of danger. He did survive, but not without the mental scars that only combat leaves you with. Not for the first time did I believe that someone was watching over our family.

Although AFCENT was wall-to-wall work for both of us, punctuated by the infrequent periods of 'something different,' the following tale was unforeseen, painful and definitely something different. As a result of a barbecue held at our house in the spring of 1984 and, after rather too much to drink, I volunteered, following an afternoon of badgering from an army chum of mine, Lt. Col. Phil Spooner, to enter the Nijmegan March. The Nijmegan March was an annual event held in Nijmegan, Holland, marching a route that was symbolic of the four loops of a clover with Nijmegan at its epicentre. Each loop was 25 miles or 45 kilometres long and each entrant had to wear military dress, including boots, but with an additional extra weight of 10kg to be strapped to their body, either around their waist or supported at the shoulders. The weight, which was checked frequently during the march, can be of any substance, but it is usually sand or salt.

After very little training, we entered as an independent duo attached to several organised teams representing AFCENT, the benefit of that being that they would feed and support us. The Nijmegan March was, historically, a training exercise for the Dutch military and dates back to 1909, but it now caters to more civilians (worldwide) than it does to the military – with the entry limited to 47,000, only about 5,000 are military teams, with the odd additions like Phil and myself. Thousands don't make it, and unfortunately some even die, but if you do complete the course, you are presented with an approved medal, the Vierdaagsekruis. I have mine framed. The march always takes place in July, the third Tuesday being day one. It's not difficult to see why there are so many casualties. After the second day's march, blood was seeping through the seams of Phil's boots! With that in mind, because my feet were also in trouble, we decided not to remove our boots until we arrived home. We were both in slippers for about three weeks and Phil required minor surgery.

When this tour drew to a close, unusually, most of me wanted it to continue. Despite the fact that a more arduous, strenuous, painful, soul-destroying tour I could not imagine – this was a 'heart and soul' tour, and I would have given anything to have it extended! Nevertheless, all good things come to an end, so Ann and I packed our bags, said our sad farewells and made our way to RAF Leuchars in Fife, Scotland. It was January 1985.

CHAPTER 13

RAF LEUCHARS

The return to the UK was an overcast affair – particularly for me. I didn't really want to leave Holland, as I've made clear, although I did need a little break. However, the real reason for my feelings of dejection was that I was returning to UK as a Flight Lieutenant! I had been a Flight Lieutenant for over seven years with, what I at least thought were two good tours under my belt. I honestly felt that with what I had achieved in Holland, I should have been returning as a Squadron Leader. A month or so earlier, I had phoned my Desk Officer at the MOD and posed a question about this – and the reply I got baffles me, even today.

It was felt that I had been out of 'real' catering for too long and needed a period of rehabilitation! Real catering? What on earth did they think I had been doing for the last four years at AFCENT? However, there was no point in arguing about it and, in any event, it wasn't the Desk Officer's fault, so I tightened my belt and tried to be positive – but I did feel a little let down, to be honest.

With hindsight, it turned out to be a good tour – albeit short. After AFCENT, Leuchars was hardly a challenge! There was a job to be done, but it didn't require my full attention. Ann quite happily got involved with a group of wives who play-acted their role in the aftermath of a nuclear attack – a sort of multi-purpose group of Florence Nightingales. They got together once a week to play-out different scenarios. They even wore overalls and 1940s tin hats with FIRST AID printed on them. The important thing was that she enjoyed it and felt that these procedures were important and so, for the first time, she didn't feel the need to seek employment elsewhere. She seemed happy.

For my part, the Sergeant in my office was also a leader in the Mountain Rescue Team, so I started to go out on their training missions into the Cairngorms and I learned a lot about mountain- and ice-climbing, orienteering and even did a bit of skiing! What was even better was that Tony, our eldest son, was still with the 45 Commandos at Arbroath, so he was able to join us on several occasions and could spend time with his mother and myself. This was really special. Ann seemed to miss the boys more and more. She certainly seemed happier when one or more of them were at home with us.

In the August of 1985, I was called up to the Station Commander's Office and informed that I had been promoted to the rank of Squadron Leader and was to be posted to RAF Kinloss in Fife, Scotland, that September. Our joy was tempered by the thought of repacking after only eight months in our present post – but, I had obviously been rehabilitated! Ann, of course, just took this in her stride. The eight-month break from the demands of her AFCENT job seemed to have given her a new lease of life. She quickly started to organise the impending move – she just required a house to move to!

CHAPTER 14

RAF KINLOSS

This move was helped considerably by the fact that I was taking over the squadron from my friend and colleague, Alan, who had been my opposite number at Hereford. Knowing how dedicated he was to detail, I had little doubt that the squadron would be running like a Swiss watch – and I wasn't disappointed! That did, of course, create a new challenge in that I had to maintain it at that level.

Of all the ranks I held in the RAF, the two ranks I was most comfortable in were Sergeant and Squadron Leader. I now believe that, in both cases, it was because these roles were the start of being a senior rank and having greater responsibilities and that required me to 'step up'. So that's what I did, and boy, oh, boy, did I love it!

It seemed to have a similar effect on Ann. She not only secured a job working for the local newspaper, which she loved, but she also went back to school with the long-term view of taking a degree in Business Studies. Both of these events were met with a completely different reaction from my Station Commander who commended Ann for deciding to improve her mind via further education, but most heartedly disapproved of her working. He, or his wife, or probably both, were still of the 'old school' view who felt that officers' wives should dedicate all of their spare time to flower arranging or other such pursuits – working was something that airmen's wives did! However, their views didn't change a thing and I made it quite clear to the Station Commander that if working made my Ann happy, then that was exactly how she was going to fill her time. We never agreed, but, fortunately, Ann was not the only wife who worked, so, over time, I believe he reluctantly slid into the twentieth century, no doubt dragging his wife kicking and screaming.

The other bit of information that came my way which helped considerably was that my boss's wife – he was the Officer Commanding the Admin Wing – had had a career as a solicitor in London and she even refused to join her husband on the station! Tut, tut! Whatever next!

Life was busy for both of us, but I don't think we've ever been happier as we were then. A little like when we were at AFCENT, we had both become immersed in our own worlds, but unlike at AFCENT, we shared everything. However, Ann had seemed a little downcast over four or five weeks, so much so that I broached the subject one evening.

"Oh! It's nothing," she said, "It's just that mid-life thing."

She went on to say that the medical officer had made an appointment for her to see a consultant at the hospital in Inverness and asked if I would drive her. So there I was, sitting in the car park outside the hospital in Inverness, wondering what was taking so long and why she had asked me to drive her.

After what seemed like a couple of hours, I decided to wander into the hospital just to see what the delay was. I hadn't even got both feet out of the car and I saw her approaching. Even at a distance of about 100 yards and with her looking down at the floor, I could tell she was crying. She was sobbing those great big sobs that come when something dreadful has happened.

She looked up at me, her eyes red from crying and said, "You can't leave me now."

"What are you saying," I said. "I've no intention of leaving you. What on earth's the matter?"

Now safely in my arms, she continued to sob, but blurted out, "I've got Parkinson's Disease!"

She clung on to me tightly and repeated, "You can't leave me now. I shall need someone to look after me."

I held her even tighter and, through tears of my own, I said, "I've got no intention of ever leaving you – we'll fight this together!"

But in that moment, I realised just how much damage I had caused her through my thoughtless affair. I swore then that I would look after her, no matter what.

The next few days were hell. I don't remember either of us stopping crying long enough to talk about the disease or its possible effects. I knew nothing about Parkinson's or its implications, but that evening, I popped across the road to speak to a chum who was also the Station Medical Officer. One look from him when he opened the door told me he knew the reason for my calling. We went into his dining room out of earshot of his family. He expressed his sorrow and said that he'd thought it was a neurological disease, but wasn't certain which one – hence the referral to the consultant at Inverness. Following my questions, he filled me in with some of the details.

Apparently, Ann had made an appointment to see him because she was aware of her writing becoming 'spidery' and how sometimes, her writing hand would shake particularly when she was sitting quietly. He went on to say that it was a progressive disease which could be controlled with drugs, but that there was no known cure. He also said that there were other symptoms to watch out for. Over time, the tremors would get worse. Her movements might slow down as a result of rigid muscles and her general mobility could be impaired. He went on to say that these were early days in her illness and the symptoms wouldn't became obvious for some time, but he was more concerned about her mental approach.

She was clearly very depressed, and anxiety and apathy usually followed a diagnosis, so she was to be careful about her decision-making.

I think I left feeling worse after hearing all this than when I'd arrived, but I was at least armed with some information. Over the next few weeks, Ann did indeed withdraw into her own world and didn't want to talk about the Parkinson's, but, otherwise, she seemed okay. She thought it sensible to hand in her notice at the newspaper, which she did, but offered them no reason for doing so. She also pulled out of her Business Studies course, again offering no explanation. She just said to me that it was none of their business. For my part, I tried to talk about the future, but she just insisted that everything would be fine.

I rang my Desk Officer at the MOD and asked if it would be possible to get a posting either in Command HQ or the MOD. My thinking was that it would be further south and that a paper-shuffling 9 to 5 job would give me more time to spend with Ann until we could make a longer term plan. The Desk Officer rang me about a week later and said that a job would become available about March/April time the following year, 1987.

Things hadn't really improved at home. Ann still didn't want to talk about her illness and insisted that I keep the problem to ourselves – which included keeping it from the boys. I thought that was wrong. I thought the boys should be told, but I agreed nevertheless.

About a week later, I brought up the subject of a move to RAF Brampton Command HQ. We had served there before and she had been very happy. She just stared at me as I rambled on about a quieter job and that we would be able to see much more of each other – not to mention that we would be able to frequent the London theatres, as we would be fairly close to the city. I also mentioned the last time we were at Brampton, when she had worked in Civilian Administration on the station and, therefore, there was a chance that she might be able to get her old job back. She continued to stare at me and then said that no one would employ her with Parkinson's Disease and, anyway, she had thought it through and she wanted me to resign my commission and leave the Air Force. Talk about unprepared – I was absolutely speechless.

Of all the possible scenarios, leaving the Air Force had not been included in my ponderings. I just sat there, trying to gather my thoughts. Of course, she had every right to ask. My service career had been her service career, so she had served almost as long as me, just in a different role. But it did, nevertheless, stop me in my tracks. In a flash, I saw my whole world crumbling around me. We were silent for some time and then I said as gently as possible, "You wouldn't like to think about Brampton, would you?"

In a matter of seconds, she absolutely flared up and screamed that she had every right to want to settle down and then, almost as suddenly, she broke down and wept, absolutely shaking, totally broken.

"Please!" she said. "I want to settle down!"

I held her in my arms, trying to soothe her. "Okay," I said, "I'll make the arrangements."

And that's what I did. For the right reasons, you can get a PVR (Premature Voluntary Release) from your service contract. You put your case, in writing, explaining why you require early retirement and wait. It's not normal for them to refuse – after all, they don't really want people who don't want to serve. But it can take up to 18 months. The higher up the ladder you are, the more difficult it is. But, as they had already offered me Brampton, I assumed that it could be done more quickly. They predicted a date of September/October in the following year, 1987. I would have been just two years in post.

CHAPTER 15

MOVING ON

The next year was the worst that I can ever remember. After over 30 years of service, I now had to find a job. I had to buy a house in a world that I'd had no contact with, and I was frightened! I tried to think of it as a challenge, but I didn't want to be challenged. I didn't want to live and work with people who didn't understand my world. All of this was made worse because Ann was also suffering, not just with the knowledge that she had Parkinson's Disease – as if that wasn't bad enough – but she also had to give up her world too, the only world she had known for nearly 30 years. And, to make matters worse, she had sworn me to secrecy. She didn't want anyone to know why we were leaving the service and that still included the boys!

This placed me in an untenable position because everyone knew that I loved the service and wouldn't voluntarily leave – so they were left to draw their own conclusions. Years later, friends, old and new, said that they didn't know what was going on – and why should they? There was only the slightest tremor in Ann's right hand and her walking pace was not so sprightly as it used to be. But to me, her sadness showed on her face – it was one that masked a troubled soul and she didn't smile quite so frequently.

For my part, I could understand her not wanting people to know and having to deal with all the sympathy that ensues, but I felt that she should have told the boys – we were a family, after all – but that was her wish. Other than the differences that I've mentioned, no one would have really guessed that she had Parkinson's and those differences were only noticed by those nearest to her who saw her on a daily basis. And, if truth be told, I only noticed them after she had been diagnosed – and possibly then, only because I was looking. I read somewhere that when a person has finally been diagnosed with Parkinson's, they experience a great sense of relief. Well, that may be true of some, but it certainly wasn't what happened in Ann's case. It turned out that in the deepest recesses of Ann's mind, she'd thought she had a brain tumour and, to her, that seemed infinitely better! For her, Parkinson's was a life sentence.

It turns out to be no great surprise that I screwed up my working life after leaving the Air Force. I don't say this as any criticism of Ann whatsoever, because her needs came first, and they were always the most important thing to me. But I never did find that career outside the RAF that I could thrive in. With hindsight, there were one or two jobs which maybe I should have taken but, alas, I didn't. In short, I resigned from my first job with Trusthouse Forte as General Manager of their premises at Heathrow's Terminal Three, and purchased a small departmental store in Dawlish in the south-west in 1988.

During those early years in Dawlish, I saw very little change in Ann's condition and it was never a subject that encouraged discussion. These were troubled years for me though. I found myself constantly worried, usually about money and the downturn in the business due to the recession, and I was frustrated with life in general, including a degree of self-pity about my lack of career achievement and anger at the world in general.

In 1992, we were certain that if we didn't get rid of the business, we would end up in the bankruptcy court. Again, this was no criticism of Ann, who had really found her place in life – she was a natural salesperson – but even she couldn't weather the storm of the recession. In many ways, I think that the lack of deterioration in her disease was due to her single-mindedness in trying to make our business a success. Throughout those early years, if you asked Ann how she was, she always answered, "I'm fine." And, although she always remained 'fine', when we finally crept out from under the debris of the business which, in the end we almost 'gave away', there seemed to be an acceleration of her symptoms.

By the middle of 1993, there was a noticeable increase in her right side tremor, but I also noticed a slight difficulty in her walking, together with what I thought was a slightly stooped posture. Most of these things were indiscernible to the casual eye, but, because I was aware of the trauma she had gone through with the loss of our business, I began looking at her more closely. She had certainly become depressed and very anxious about the future.

It was at this time, after much coaxing, that I got her to 'declare' her problem, if you like, publicly and to consult a doctor. By 1993, she was in the incredibly safe hands of Dr. Vaughn Pearce at Exeter (Wonford) Hospital. That was also the same year we managed to put enough money together to buy an apartment in Dawlish called, 'The Clint', which was to be our home for the next 11 years.

As it turned out, those 11 years were not just the happiest that I can remember – perhaps as they were the essence of what Ann thought of as 'settling down' – but because we knew her disease was in the safe hands of Vaughn Pearce and his colleagues, who with almost a minimum of fuss, were able to control Ann's deterioration with the right balance of drugs, which can only come from years of experience. I will forever be indebted to Dr Pearce and his team in the Movement Disorder Service.

By 2004, although there were now marked signs of deterioration, for someone who had had nearly 20 years of Parkinson's Disease, Ann was in remarkably good shape, thanks to constant monitoring of her condition. And, of course, when asked how she was, she was always "fine."

Those 11 years from 1993 to 2004 were also productive years. In 1994, we were able to purchase a small seasonal business in Dawlish Warren that sold not just summer stuff, but also papers, cigarettes and even alcohol. For Ann – and me too – this was a godsend. It was a small, manageable business, operating from Easter to Halloween on a renewable lease. It never turned over more than £40,000 a year, but Ann loved it. My jobs were to sort out the early papers and organise the milk, but, otherwise, it was all Ann's doing. I would spend a good deal of my day with her, but it also meant that I could slip away for a game of golf!

In 1995, the owner of the shop, who also owned the very large caravan park that it was attached to, asked me if I would consider running a barbecue on a Friday and Saturday evening for all the holidaymakers. I agreed and, for the next four years, Ann and I worked hand in glove running a small, but lucrative shop and a barbecue business which turned over about £500-£600 in cash every week!

At the end of the 1998 season though, we hung up our boots and retired. We didn't really miss it. The seasons had got busier and, every year, Ann was just a little bit wearier and we were both closing in on 60 years of age. Although tired at times, that was a decade and a bit where we never stopped smiling. We lived in a circle of love that was impenetrable from the outside world. The following year, we celebrated 40 years of marriage and, other than a few mishaps on my part, I wouldn't have missed a moment of it.

CHAPTER 16

THE STORM

Over the next few years, the signs were that there could be possible problems in living in a first floor apartment for somebody with a progressive disability. We considered many possibilities, not least an external lift – but even with some financial assistance, it was still going to cost us about £20,000. After looking at various different options that might help us to stay in our apartment, eventually the sheer convenience of living at ground level meant that we, rather reluctantly, decided to sell. In the spring of 2004, when the deal was done, we had lived in 39 properties in 16 counties in the UK and four countries abroad, yet a quarter of our married life had been spent there at 'The Clint' in Dawlish, Devon.

Just as a tongue-in-cheek aside – during the football season of 1996, Ann rang me from the shop, so excited.

"I've won the pools!" she cried, through a mixture of tears and excitement. Ann used to do a 'line' in one of the large football pools, which she did on a renewable 10-week cycle, and she always used the same numbers.

"Are you sure?" I asked her.

"Yes, yes!" she said. "I've checked in the paper and I've got all the numbers!"

"I'll come down," I said. When I arrived at the shop, she was crying.

"What on earth's the matter?" I asked. She looked up and waved her coupon at me. "I forgot to post it – the old one expired last week!"

She was absolutely inconsolable, not for herself, but because of what it could have done for the boys. I rang the Pools helpline and, sure enough, along with a Naval Petty Officer, they had won a £2.1 million jackpot, of which £987,000 would have been Ann's. Apparently, the Petty Officer had a different configuration, so would have won more. As it turned out, he won much more! Ho hum!

The actual move from 'The Clint' was a little more frantic than I had intended. Within weeks of advertising the place, an offer was made by two doctors who lived in London. It was an offer too good to refuse, but they wanted to move in quickly. It didn't give us any time to look for a new home, so we decided to rent. I think the idea was that we could spend the next year deciding where we wanted to live. I always wanted to live in Teignmouth, another small seaside town adjoining Dawlish, but Ann was ambivalent. So, at the July of

2004, after some minor alterations, we moved into a newly-renovated ground floor, two-bedroomed rented apartment right on the sea front in Dawlish, called Marine Parade. In so many ways, it seemed ideal. It was walking distance from shops, doctors and dentists, plus rail and bus services. It was considerably smaller than 'The Clint', but of a similar period – the mid 1850s. It was sort of twee! And it was rather nice just to walk out of the front door and have the sea front on our doorstep.

However, on the evening of the 27th October that year, a day I am never likely to forget, disaster struck! We were told afterwards that it was a combination of autumn tides, a freak storm out at sea and just bad luck! "It's the first time this has happened for 200 years," was the quote from the council/environmental agency. The storm hit without warning. The waves initially were so high and so forceful that they ripped the cladding off the front of the building. Even with all the help that I was able to muster and the use of sandbags and so on, within 20 minutes, the force of water had buckled the front door and shoved aside the sandbags like so many bags of feathers. Ann had moved upstairs to our neighbours, having rescued the cats. I stood on the stairs, absolutely helpless as the storm tore into our apartment. I did think that if I opened the back door and lifted the cover off a large sewer which I knew was situated there that I might be able to reduce the level of water in the apartment. It turned out that I needed help to remove the cover, which took a little time, only to find that the old Victorian drains were too narrow to take that amount of water, so it quickly washed back, excrement included! The water level finally settled at about three feet. By this time, the storm had almost ripped off the front door, so the river ran inside unheeded. With the help of a couple of other people, whose names I never found out, we waded through the apartment to see if anything could be saved but, sad to say, it was all too late! In 20 minutes, Mother Nature had destroyed 90% of our possessions and our lives would never be the same again.

The couple living above us very kindly put us up for a couple of nights until I could sort out alternative accommodation. The following morning, the devastation was mind-boggling and total. The water had subsided during the night and what was left was a mass of furniture, soft furnishings, ornaments, clothing, photographs and special things massed together in a grotesque heap covered in excrement, dead birds and the debris of the sea – nothing looked salvageable. But over and above this sea of desolation was the pervading smell of the sewer. I knew that I should be strong for so many reasons, but I wasn't. I lowered my head and wept.

Having pulled myself together, I went upstairs, looked at Ann, held her in my arms and said, "I think we've lost everything."

She held me tight and replied, "Don't worry. They're only things – we're safe and that's all that matters."

I held her at arm's length and she gave me a weak smile. Her demeanour clearly belied her statement but, nevertheless, this was one extraordinary woman that had found a strength that eluded me.

The destruction was total. Even our car, which had been parked on the forecourt, was a write-off. The total amount finally agreed by our insurers was £27,000, which was less than we wanted, especially as the car which was given a value of £2,200 had been purchased for £5,000 six months earlier! But you cannot negotiate forever. Also, there had been some fearsome arguments regarding the value of some antiques. I managed to get replacement invoices for some pieces, but there was considerable scepticism from the insurers. But we eventually compromised – in their favour!

During all of this process, we had rented a furnished holiday home which strangely enough was opposite 'The Clint' in Mayflower Close, but it was convenient. Also, a friend of mine had loaned me his spare car. We stayed in the holiday home for four months – time enough, they thought, for the property to dry out and to be redecorated and re-carpeted. We moved back in with minimum furniture as we were unsure of how long we would be there, so we didn't want to purchase furniture that would be of no use when we finally settled down.

This was a really trying time. Both of us seemed to be living on our nerves and Ann's illness seemed to have escalated in a short time. We sought help and were informed that great stress can sometimes do just that, but were equally assured that her symptoms should ease when we settled again. The escalation in Ann's illness was, with hindsight, a reflection of my own symptoms – anxiety, frustration and anger – all, as usual, taken out on my nearest and dearest. Add depression, stress and in my case, a huge sense of loss to the mix and you have all the constituent parts of a time bomb! Ann was more understanding than me, but even she threatened to leave me twice during the period we were in the holiday home and the first couple of months back in our storm-ridden apartment.

For my part, I could not get over the huge, pervading sense of loss. I seemed to blame everybody, particularly the insurers, for their tardiness, the council for their apathetic support and help and their constant denial that if the main sewers/drains had been kept clear of debris, which they weren't, a lot of damage could have been avoided. I also felt upset at the landlord for telling us that the apartment was habitable, only to find that damp was fast appearing in the guise of salt crystals on just about every wall. It turned out that, because of the age of the building, with it being from circa 1860, the walls were like sponges and, realistically, the flat would have taken about a year to dry out. But I think the landlord was trying to be kind. Unfortunately, it just added fuel to my fast-approaching time bomb.

It exploded one evening in April when, after a blistering row, I walked out, leaving Ann in tears. I spent the night walking the coastline, wishing I would die! Something happened during that night or, to be precise, nearer to dawn. I found myself walking along the Exeter

Canal, just outside the city of Exeter, and I was soaking wet. I'm not sure that I remember how I got there, but I sat down on the wet grass and cried. I seemed to cry for ages – all the pain and anguish of the last six or seven months just pouring out of me in huge, body-shaking sobs. When I finally stopped, I realised that I was only crying for my loss, for me! How could I have so easily forgotten that Ann must have suffered every bit as much as me – and she had a degenerative disease! A sudden feeling of self-loathing washed over me. How had I become such a selfish, self-centred, egotistical bastard? Although I couldn't bear myself at that time, I knew that I had to get back to Ann to explain, to plead, to tell her that I was now alright and, that if she took me back and –, not for the first time – forgave me, that I would put things right.

I rushed as fast as my legs would carry me. I had walked out without money, keys or a phone and I was impeded by my soaking wet clothing. I arrived home about 06.00 or 07.00 hrs, I think. It was just getting light. I waited outside the apartment. Fortunately, there weren't too many people about and those that were certainly weren't interested in me. I was unsure as to whether to knock or wait until I saw movement. The curtains were still open from the previous night, so I wasn't even sure Ann was in – she could have called one of the boys! That thought made me feel even worse. I was just about to walk away, thinking I'd leave it for another hour, when the front door opened. She just half-smiled and opened her arms. I fell into them and hugged her. I tried to talk, but then I started crying again. And then I realised she was too.

After what seemed an age, we released our grip on each other and, with tear-stained faces, we both tried to speak. I tried to say how sorry I was, but she interrupted me and said that it was just as much her fault, but she had been so worried about me and that she was just about to ring the boys because she didn't know what else to do. We went indoors and I hugged her again and tried to express how sorry I was and that it would never happen again. She put her finger to my lips and said, "We are both to blame and we will both put it right!" She went on to say that, starting today, we would start looking for somewhere to live, "preferably on a hill," she smiled.

I just hugged and hugged her until she reminded me that I was soaking wet and so too was she now, and that if we didn't change, we'd both probably end up with pneumonia!

That morning I vowed to myself that I would somehow make up for the wrongs that I had inflicted on her and that such bad behaviour would never be repeated. I also vowed that, in future, I would put her first – in all things. I realised that it would be a long time before I would be able to forgive myself, if ever.

CHAPTER 17

FROM THE FRYING PAN...

The next couple of months were just 'full on'. Almost every day we were out, either viewing properties or collecting paperwork on what we thought were suitable ones. We decided that we would concentrate our search in Teignmouth – a town we had always loved and there now seemed little reason not to move there. After all, it was only three miles from Dawlish. We viewed so many properties, we almost began to despair. On top of all the usual problems of purchasing a property, our main question was could it flood? For all the obvious reasons, the common cause of looking for a property had brought us even closer together and completely dispelled the memory of that April – well, almost.

I think maybe I was still looking for some physical signs of her deterioration and, alas, they were there.

Of course, this just heightened my feelings of guilt. She walked with a little more difficulty now, her balance was poorer, there was a tight rigidity to her facial muscles which almost gave her a masked look and this was also coupled with her staring almost as though her thoughts were elsewhere. To my mind, her voice had also become softer and, at times, it was difficult to hear her. It was also about this time that I noticed the early signs of dyskinesia (shaking) in her right side. None of these things were discussed, but I did try and shield her when we were in company, particularly company she didn't know very well. I knew that if she thought people were aware of her symptoms and made their awareness known, she would have been terribly distressed. However, it's worth mentioning that I was probably overly concerned about her physical differences because it was now well-known amongst our circle of close friends that she had Parkinson's Disease, even though it was rarely discussed. Unbeknownst to our friends their support and the sheer act of treating her as normal, made her normal!

Two of our closest friends, David and Sue, with whom we holidayed for well over two decades, never did anything but treat Ann as normal – although she always feared that she would lose their friendship, which, of course, never happened. When her dyskinesia became so bad it was clearly obvious, David even turned it into a joke, suggesting that he could make better use of her shaking hand! This may sound lewd, but, believe me, when you can reduce a disability to fun and laugh about it, that's medicine in the making.

By June of 2005, we had purchased what we thought was an ideal property called 'Campion' in Teignmouth. It was a ground floor apartment in an old Victorian house. It did require some work, but, by the end of June, we had moved in. It was everything that we hoped for in that it was spacious with delightful distant views of the River Exe. We had two wonderful summers there. It was, alas, during our time at 'Campion' that we realised that it wouldn't be forever. Ann's disability moved up a notch or two. Her balance had become so poor that I had to have handholds installed to enable her to get from the bedroom to the bathroom. She also required holds in the bathroom. Walking had also become really difficult for her, so we purchased a 'buggy' to help get her around. We had also added a walking stick to her growing list of aids. Even with all of the problems I've listed, if it had not been for the following event, we would probably have struggled on there.

During the winter of 2006/7, I was struck down with an ailment which confined me to my bed for four or five days. It was during that period that we realised how cut off we were. When you pulled into the car park of 'Campion' to access our garage, it was still about 100-120 yards to our front door – and it was all downhill. So, for Ann to access her buggy, which also had to be kept and powered up in the same garage, it was almost impossible for her to get to it without help. We knew we could contact friends for assistance, but that would never do as a 'forever arrangement'. So, reluctantly, we realised we needed to move to a property which was suitable for someone with Ann's problems, but also close to the road.

Once again, we looked at so many properties, but none seemed ideal, bearing in mind that we were hoping that this would be our last move! Just on the off-chance, one Sunday in February, I decided to pop round to the few estate agents in Teignmouth that were open – and there weren't many. I was just about to give up when, leaving the last of three agents, the girl on duty dashed out and called me back in. She said that there was a property being renovated on the left-hand side, just up the Exeter Road. She had no details, but she knew that the property, an old Victorian house, was being divided into apartments and would eventually be for sale. The property was called 'Magnolia House' and it was exactly a quarter of a mile from the town centre on the left, facing Teignmouth Community College. Geographically, it was perfect. Set back off the road and no more than five to 10 minutes walking distance to town. When I popped around to see it though, it was still a building site, and quite obviously needing a lot of work externally and as it turned out, having peeked through the front door windows, internally as well. I was just about to leave, having decided that it was probably not worth pursuing, when a chap rushed out of the front door of the house and asked if he could help. He seemed very pleasant and was only too happy to answer my questions. With that, he was joined by a lady of similar age (about mid to late 40s). They were absolutely bubbling over with enthusiasm about their building project.

I stood and looked at the project with them. The house had been built in about 1830-40 and it was a traditional smallish Georgian/Victorian villa. Off to the right, facing the house, which pointed north, was a large modern extension which, I was informed, was a self-contained three-bedroomed 'wing' with its own garden. I quickly pointed out that I was only interested in ground floor accommodation with no stairs and explained our circumstances. Well, they were suddenly both gushing about how lucky I was then. They went on to say that the first apartment to be finished would be the ground floor one with two bedrooms and with something a little extra special. The man ushered me into the house, which, as I'd noticed when gazing through the door, was a building site, but clearly work was in progress. We turned right off the entrance hall and through what he told me would be our front door. We entered what must have been a large Victorian drawing/sitting room. It probably looked larger because it was empty, but I estimated that it must have been 16-18 feet wide and at least 24 feet long. On my right were two large windows reaching from my waist up to about one foot from the ceiling, which I was informed was twelve feet high. The windows faced east. Opposite them was a large original fireplace and, again, this was about six feet long with a high mantle. Through the rubble, I could see perfection! The other rooms, all of small to moderate size, were ideal as they formed a crescent around the top of the sitting room. I visualised, just by putting up hand-holds, that Ann would be able to access all the other rooms with little trouble.

The something a little extra special was a large veranda which would be accessed through what was listed as the second bedroom. At that time, all you could see through the window was a large area of about 9 by 16 feet, of what was clearly the flat roof of one of the rooms which would become a basement apartment. He went on to tell me how and where the door would be knocked through, giving us access, and that it would be written into our lease, giving us legal ownership of it.

As I wandered around, I could see through the rubble and mess and became quite excited. I told them that I would like to return in a couple of days with Ann and possibly one of our sons. The happy façade seemed to slip for a second and he pointed out, quite angrily I thought, that unless I committed, he could well sell it to someone else. I pointed out to him that I could hardly commit without my wife seeing it, but I was very interested. And then, just as suddenly, the happy smiling face was back.

"Of course, of course," he said, smiling. "I was just being overly eager! No, no – that's fine," he went on to say, "we'll see you in a couple of days then?" I said that I would inform the estate agents that I was interested and would return on Tuesday afternoon about 14.00 hrs.

On my way back home, although excited regarding my find, I wondered about the sudden change in his demeanour. Had I seen something that was important? This chap was, after all, going to be the freeholder. But, no, I rationalised that such a big project must come with a lot of pressure and that what I had seen was just the anxiety that he might lose the sale. Nevertheless, it did make me think.

When I was a child, we – my mother, brother and sister (our father had died in 1942) – lived, or rented to be precise, the downstairs part of a house in Cricklewood in London. The house was owned by German Jews who had fled the persecution of the Nazi's during the Second World War. Ideally, they wanted the use of the whole house, but, back in the 1940s and 50s, if a property was purchased and part of it was being rented, the only way that the owners could gain access to the whole place was to find suitable alternative accommodation for their tenants. It wasn't just their responsibility, but the council also had a responsibility of rehousing tenants too – but that could take time. So it was in the interest of the owners to find 'suitable' properties. In 1951 or 52 (I'm not really sure when), the owners told my mother that they had secured a flat in Notting Hill, which is in West London. We were in the north-west, and not being a million miles away, my mother decided to go and view it. She always told us that she had decided against it before she'd even gone in, however, she decided that she should at least have a look. Primarily, she said that the overall appearance was 'seedy' and that it seemed to be 'propped up' at one side – it was semi-detached. A bespectacled gentleman greeted her and something about his manner made her feel uneasy. Also, she went on to say that the passage from the front door 'tilted' to the right, which probably explained the 'prop'. He asked her if she would like a cup of tea and she noticed that the kitchen was the warmest room. She said that the moment she entered the house, she felt ill at ease. She didn't know why, but there was the most awful smell about the place and she apparently decided that she needed to get out. She turned to go, but found that the gentleman was between her and the front door.

"I've got to go!" she said loudly and, in the same instant, she took hold of his right arm and pushed him sideways as forcefully as she could. She said that she ran out of the house, leaving the doors open and that she didn't stop running until she got to the high street. She had no idea why.

In June 1953, John Cristie of 10 Rillington Place, Notting Hill was hanged for murdering six females who he'd secreted behind the walls of his kitchen. It looks as though my mother's instincts paid off. That same instinct, unfortunately, wasn't passed from mother to son!

On the Tuesday afternoon, as arranged at 14.00 hrs, Ann, myself and Tony, our eldest son, returned to view the apartment in Magnolia House. Once again, we were met by the same chap, this time on his own. I introduced Tony and Ann to him and asked him if it was alright if we went around on our own and, that if there were any questions, we'd catch him afterwards. He seemed to get a little agitated and suggested that he needed to be there because he was the freeholder. Frankly, I thought that was nonsense, but I went on to say that he'd shown me around the last time and, unless something had changed, there wasn't much more that he could add, other than questions we might have after our viewing.

He became quite indignant saying he was only trying to help and, "anyway," he went on, "it is still a building site and, therefore, visitors have to be accompanied."

That kind of made sense, but I still thought it was unnecessary.

"Okay," I said, reluctantly, "lead on."

He gushed all the way around about what he was going to do, how he would change everything that we wanted him to and would paint the various rooms in colours of our liking. In fact, everything we suggested, he agreed to. He did point out that, depending on what we wanted, there might be a slight additional cost. However, he quickly went on to say that as his team would do the work under his guidance, he would undercut any other quotes and the work would be finished to a very high standard. Although I found him a little over-sensitive regarding some of the details that we wanted – in particular the access to the terrace and cutting through the wall between the bedroom and bathroom to make the main bedroom en suite – he very quickly pointed out that he'd been developing properties for years and was highly thought of and would work with us at all times.

Both Ann and I thought the property to be ideal, both in size and location, and, with the promise of our own outside space beyond the second bedroom, it seemed perfect. In view of Ann's slight, but noticeable, deterioration in her health, it was an opportunity to almost customise our apartment. The seller informed us that it would take a couple of months, but should be ready to move in by August 2007.

After we left, the three of us went into Teignmouth for a coffee to talk through what we'd seen and what we'd agreed, prior to going to the estate agent.

As soon as we sat down, Ann said, "That man is going to be trouble. I wouldn't trust him any further than I could throw him!" Tony and I both looked at her in astonishment.

"Why?" I asked. "He seemed fine to me. He was a little over-sensitive," I said, "but that could work in our favour in terms of the standard of his work."

Tony agreed and went on to say that it might just be a case of staying 'on top' of the project in order to make sure we were getting what we paid for.

Ann went on to say that she liked the apartment, or my vision of it, but she definitely didn't like him. She was still very uneasy about him as we were driving away.

"You mark my words," she said. "He's going to be trouble."

There was no point in arguing with her. It was, after all, only women's intuition!

Oh, my God! How I wished I'd listened to her! As we did with 'The Clint', we sold the property on Buckeridge Avenue promptly, but again they wanted to move in quickly. So, once again, simply because we didn't want to lose the sale, we rented. This time, bearing in mind the new apartment was supposed to be ready within two months, we rented a large caravan on a holiday site just outside Teignmouth and put all of our furniture into storage. Over the next two to three months, we needed fairly regular access to our new apartment – which was always done by appointment – mainly to check the work that had to be completed before we moved in and for Sharps to redesign the master bedroom and redesign the second bedroom as a study. I hired a company to design and make drapes for the sitting room, bearing in mind the drapes had a ten foot drop and required at least six to eight weeks to make. As well as curtains and blinds for all the other rooms, the flat required carpeting, plus a host of features that needed to be installed for Ann's safety. None of this was achieved, as I have said, without an appointment and, even then, the seller would follow both me and whoever I had brought in to complete these tasks, muttering all the time about how he could do the job better and cheaper and that we were just throwing our money away and that I should listen to the voice of experience! I always tried to pacify him and point out that the work had to be done by specialists and they could easily work in harmony with his team, but I'm afraid that sentiment rarely worked and he certainly scared off a couple of tradesmen who weren't prepared to work under such conditions.

You would think I would have woken up to the fact that something wasn't quite right – but I didn't! We had several serious rows about his interference, but I always ended up convincing myself that the apartment was perfect for us and that he was simply under extreme pressure to achieve the deadline. Hence I always tried to find another solution, which usually meant that some of the work that I needed to be done had to be postponed.

All of this took its toll on both of us, particularly Ann, who also found it difficult living in the confined space of a caravan. By September, we were informed that all work was completed, and it was only one month late – which, of course, was our fault because we had interfered with his work flow! Contracts were completed, but we still needed work done before we could move in. Carpets had to be laid and drapes, curtains and blinds had to be hung. Fortunately, Sharps had been 'allowed in' the previous week, so everything was in place within a few days of completion. However, outside our apartment door, it was still a building site and looked like the aftermath of a warzone! When I complained about the difficulties in accessing our apartment, I was told it was our fault because we had pressurised him to finish our apartment at the expense of all the other work! Although I began to think that Ann's intuitions were coming true, I still felt that an element of what he said was true and that we should give him the benefit of the doubt.

We finally moved in the middle of October, nearly two months past the agreed deadline! However, things seemed to go badly from day one. Over and above the work that he had to do to comply with the agreed standards of handover, we had also asked him to create a doorway from the bedroom giving us direct access to the bathroom, to redecorate the whole property, which he thought unnecessary as it was redecorated only six months previously – in pink! – and, we wanted to know when the terrace was going to be built. He assured us that it would happen soon, but that it was just a bigger job than he first thought. Anyway, in its absence, we needed a hole cut through the wall to install a cat flap so that the cats could access the gardens.

About a fortnight after we had moved in, he gave me the invoice for his labours for all the aforementioned work totalling £5,178.50, which, of course, was complete nonsense. Even to give him the benefit of the doubt, it couldn't possibly have come to more than £2,000. So I went ballistic! In short, I told him that he was never going to be paid such an amount and that, by my reckoning, it could not have been more than £2,000 to £2,500 and that even the greater of these two figures was stretching credibility. He went on to say that I had forgotten that these were 'bespoke' workmen and, therefore, their hourly rate was much higher! I threw him and his invoice out and recommended that he re-think the invoice or I would take legal action against him. A few days later, a letter was pushed under our door. It stated that there had been a major problem with the workmen's timesheets, which he had now corrected, and that the total amount owed was £2,400! It also contained a separate note requesting the maintenance which was due in advance – the sum being £750 per annum. I reluctantly agreed to the £2,400, but argued that the maintenance was to cover work that couldn't possibly be met, i.e. garden maintenance, property maintenance, window cleaning and so on, and that I would pay him £250 to cover the first four months, but that I wished to see the policy for the house insurance, which was also supposed to be included in our maintenance and proof that the other tenant, his lady friend, was also paying! I went on to say that no other monies would be paid to him until there were signs that the work to be done for the benefit of common usage – i.e. gardens, car parking, access to the front door and work on the foyer so that we had better access to our own front door within the property – would be completed.

Christmas came and went with little progress, but we did receive regular letters pushed under our door, threatening us with expulsion, legal action and, that the next time we were both out, he would prevent us from getting back in! We decided that it was time to get the police involved. Unfortunately, all of this aggravation had the most damaging effect on Ann. On top of all her usual problems, we now saw heightened agitation and nervousness. This frequently surfaced as fear, which appeared at almost any noise, or the sight of this man – or even the

FROM THE FRYING PAN...

possible sight of him – with tears usually following for lengthy periods. I don't think that I have ever felt quite so frustrated in my life. In some ways, we were both frightened of him. He became so unpredictable. I wasn't frightened for myself, only for what he might do.

The letters requesting money became more frequent. One letter told us that we weren't allowed visitors anymore as it was a registered building site and he was responsible for visitors' safety! There was no reasoning with him. If I approached him, he would take my photograph which, he said, would be evidence at a court case concerning my personal abuse against him. I tried several times to reason with him, but it always ended up the same – he was right and I was wrong and that he would see me in court.

I tried to explain the damage all this was doing to Ann, but he would just look straight through me and always said that I had brought it upon myself. Having already talked it through with Colin, our middle son, who was now a police detective, I had been made aware that none of his actions were criminal, but civil and so, therefore, the police's hands were tied. To be fair, the police did try to speak to him on several occasions, but he either refused or it was through closed doors. And when they were face-to-face, he always took their photograph as evidence of their harassment and apparently, this would also be used in the forthcoming court case! Ann and I spent hours and hours with the police and found out that this man was well known in the county for abusive and threatening behaviour to almost anybody who disagreed with him. His police file was about two inches thick!

By early 2008, Ann's health had deteriorated significantly, mainly due to increased falls, but there was a noticeable deterioration in her cognitive behaviour and also memory loss too. She was referred for a neuropsychological assessment at Frenchay Hospital in Bristol. I have to say that, at the time, I blamed this man for the seeming escalation of her symptoms. The outcome of this assessment was not good, but it did open up the possibility of deep brain surgery which, at that time, seemed like a light at the end of the tunnel. We were informed that it would be a very long process. Not only did they have to get the approval for funding the operation, but it would also require several short stays at Frenchay Hospital for further detailed assessments. It was thought at that time that Ann would be an ideal candidate for such surgery.

Just prior to this news, it looked as though a lifeline had been thrown to us. Who says there's not a God in heaven? We had received notification that a Mr Down had purchased both the south apartment and the north basement which was immediately beneath us. It struck me that if the owner had to sell the apartments in their unfinished state, that might go some way to explaining his appalling behaviour during the previous six months. The financial quagmire of business was still ever present, in my mind, from the loss of our own one, however, my next thought was that hopefully it meant that Mr Grey was now going to be moving out of our lives a little. How wrong can you be?

Grey, of course, still retained ownership of the north apartment and the freehold of the whole building, and so took up permanent residence. Nevertheless, I still reasoned that the property had more leaseholders and therefore, also, a greater say in matters! In short, our army was larger. Four of the five apartments were now privately owned and both Ann and I liked Mr Down straight away. He was forthright and down-to-earth, but there was a certain honesty about him, in Ann's words. I held my counsel!

As the seller was still the freeholder and our purchase included an agreement to convert the roof of the downstairs extension – which was of course now owned by Mr Down – into our terrace, we thought this would still be feasible. Not so, according to the seller, with a slight look of triumph in his eyes. He said that Mr Down would not allow him to convert the roof of 'his' property and, in any event, he had run out of money! He went on to say that any further negotiations would have to be with Mr. Down and any conversion would have to be funded by Ann and myself. That was clearly impossible, so we had to settle for doing without – for me, this was a bitter pill to take. I had wanted the outside space so badly for Ann, knowing that, in the future, her ability to access the gardens, without help, would be impossible. In view of what I thought was Mr Down's unhelpful attitude, I must say that my heart hardened towards him. However, without funding, it was all a bit academic anyway.

The beginning of 2008 saw Mr Down attack the basement apartment with a vengeance. It was heartening to see so much activity. He had a small team – himself, his son and a hired man, but they seemed to do the work of 10 men. They were everywhere and the noise was fearsome. To be fair to Mr Down, he always kept us informed of what he was doing, offering to show us the work-in-progress and he was always apologising for the noise. We saw little of Mr Grey during that first quarter of 2008, but were still very conscious of his presence.

Ann was attending Exeter hospital on a quarterly basis and receiving individual and first class care from Dr Pearce and his team. During 2008, Ann had two more appointments at Frenchay Hospital, one requiring a three-day stay. As it happened, the stay turned out quite badly. Ann telephoned me at home to collect her and when I arrived, she was clearly upset and wanted to go home. I spoke to the consultant, the doctor in charge and the senior nurse, who all seemed to think that Ann had been a little disruptive, but she had finally co-operated enough to give them the information they needed. The consultant took me to one side and said that they needed time to look carefully at all of the information they had gained and would contact us as soon as possible. I never did quite get to the bottom of why Ann was so upset, but I gathered it had something to do with some tests she had had to undergo. Also, the admission of other patients onto the ward, who were in various stages of post-neurological brain surgery, clearly upset her. We didn't hear from them again until early 2009.

By March of 2008, Mr Down had made huge in-roads into the conversion of the basement apartment and now wanted to start work on the south apartment. Unfortunately, that required a confrontation with the original developer who was still using the south apartment to store all of his belongings. In any event, he had to be approached. He, of course, refused outright to co-operate. The battle lines had been drawn and, with little choice, we joined Mr Down's army. The next six months were pure hell. By May of that year, Mr Down had applied for something called a Tort Order, legally ordering the seller to remove his chattels from the south apartment. Prior to that though, during the night, Grey had bulldozed several tons of mud down the stairway into the north basement apartment. The weight of the mud completely blocked the interior entrance. Although the police were involved on almost a daily basis, nothing hindered Grey's vengeful quest. During this time, Ann and I were receiving letters almost on a daily basis, either threatening us or pointing to items on the lease, and conditions which, according to Grey, we had infringed. Every time I tried to speak to him, he would photograph me and then retreat into his apartment. This always preceded a visit from the police who had been informed by Grey that I had threatened him and that he was in fear of his life.

If we left windows open, he would hosepipe water in and then tell the police that he was fulfilling his duties as freeholder and cleaning the windows and he hadn't noticed that some were open! If it wasn't water, he would use his leaf blower right outside our open windows and blow in all the dust and debris he could. And, again, he would then inform the police that he was fulfilling his duties as freeholder!

Twice, he fouled the front door lock so that Ann and I were locked out. On those occasions, we had to break a window to free the lock and then had the expense of replacing the window and changing the lock. On all occasions, there was no evidence though, and when he was approached by the police, he threatened to sue them for harassment!

With the access to the basement now completely blocked, all other work for Mr Down ceased. All his labourers were now trying to clear away the mud and to repair the damage. This clearly put him back weeks. When it was finally cleared, the damage to the door, doorway and interior was immense and very costly. Of the Tort Order that he so badly needed to clear the south, there was still no sign. Mr Down completed all the work, repairing the damage to the basement only to find that when he arrived one morning the whole property had been flooded! Grey's explanation to the police was that his washing machine had malfunctioned and accidentally flooded the downstairs property without his knowledge! I have no idea how Mr Down managed to contain himself. Ann and I were at our wits' end without experiencing anything like the grief that Grey inflicted upon Mr Down, but, somehow, the man bounced back and carried on. It said an awful lot about Robert Down!

By early June 2008, the Tort Order arrived and Grey had seven days to remove his rubbish from the south apartment. Previously, in the May of the same year, Grey had tried to take out an injunction against Mr Down and his son for physical abuse and threatening behaviour. The case went to the Magistrates' Court in Plymouth and failed. But, as a result of all the evidence that had been collated by Mr Down to defend himself, it was felt that there was a case to answer against Grey, so the case was referred to the Crown Court at Exeter in July 2008. It was at that point that we became legally involved.

During the two months between May and the court case in July, Grey asked to speak to Ann and myself. I could see no reason not to see him, but, for the life of me, I couldn't imagine what he could want. Once again, he came in the company of the owner of the upstairs apartment who, for some obscure reason, still believed in him. It was a very short visit. He wanted Ann and myself to join him to fight his corner against Mr Down! I was so stunned I was almost lost for words. I just propelled him towards the door, my closing comments being, as I shut the door in his face, that I would do anything in my power to help Mr Down. The harassment continued with letters and threats during June and early July 2008. But, by July, Mr Down, myself and all the others who had become embroiled with Grey had put together what we thought was a good case against him, and I said I would certainly testify.

The case was lengthy, trying and seemingly a bit one-sided. Grey had asked for an ambulance to take him to hospital for what he said was a heart attack brought on by the stress of the possible hearing, so the case was tried, in his absence, much to his disgust, but it was, once again, adjourned until Grey could attend to defend himself at a later date – which, as it turned out, was to be a year later in July 2009. It nevertheless did feel like a victory and now we had even more time to gather evidence.

Grey spent three days in hospital with the self-imposed heart attack and was released with a clear bill of health. He finally removed all his rubbish from the south apartment in late July 2008, having informed the court that both his health and the court case had prevented him from doing so earlier. With nowhere else for his rubbish to go, it joined the rest of the rubbish on the forecourt, making it now almost impossible to access the front door from the road. I asked him a couple of times to clear a pathway through, so we could access the front door with a little more ease. The car was, of course, being parked on the main road. When he finally spoke, he just said that I had brought it on myself by joining the wrong team. I spoke once again to the police, who yet again pointed out that it was a civil matter, but they did suggest that I speak to the fire brigade through the county council. It worked. Both the council and the fire brigade informed him that he was in breach of safety regulations and that the rubbish presented a hazard to both fire and ambulance vehicles attending a call and to all the people that lived within the property. So, following several threatening letters regarding the consequences of my actions, he finally removed all the rubbish from the forecourt to the grounds in front of the south apartment.

In the September of 2008, Grey, once again, flooded the basement apartment, using the same excuse of a faulty washing machine. Following the flooding, Grey then fouled the locks of both the front and rear entrances to prevent access. He also parked a small car at the top of the stairs of the basement, so access was impossible. This, as it turned out, was Grey's first criminal act. Robert photographed the incident as part of the evidence for the forthcoming court case and this single act contributed to Grey's final downfall. The onslaught from Grey continued, but was aimed mostly at Robert Down – he did almost anything he could to halt the renovations. He complained to building control about Mr Down's working practices – which, of course, had no foundation – but it did require investigating. He also complained to the water board, British Gas and the electricity company again, about Mr Down's work ethic – all of which, again, had no foundation, but did require a response – and which, of course, created further delays!

Nevertheless, by the November (and this is the highlight of 2008), Grey was declared a bankrupt and Robert was 'offered' the purchase of the north apartment and the freehold of Magnolia House from the receivers. This, was a lengthy legal process, so November was just the start of proceedings, and Robert had to find the funds, but Grey had to move out!

CHAPTER 18

A MIXED YEAR

Early 2009 saw Ann back at Frenchay Hospital for further tests which once again required a short stay for her. She was in hospital for two nights and underwent intensive tests for about two and a half days. The summary of that report which we received in mid-February 2009 was as follows (by this time, Ann had had Parkinson's Disease for 23 years):

> *It was noted that her symptoms had become progressively worse. In particular, her mobility and her proneness to falls. Her cognitive functions had worsened. She had difficulty with recent memory and tended to lose track. She had difficulty putting thoughts together into speech. She was frequently disorientated, particularly in the mornings. Personality*

changes were noted and she could become irritable. She related this to her frustration about her condition. It was noted that the previous year's disruption was undoubtedly part of the reason for her decline. Although consistently showing a brave face, she experienced feelings of low mood, frustration and anxiety about the future. Mrs Dean had difficulty with attentional tasks and made a large number of errors and her response times were highly variable. She did appear to have some physical difficulties with tasks as a result of her motor problems. Her verbal memory was in the low range.

There were more comments, but the closing statement was thus:

Mrs. Dean's neuropsychological assessment suggests significant impairments that are consistent with her history of Parkinson's Disease. Her cognitive problems are also consistent with her Parkinson's Disease. There was no real evidence of dementia, so from a purely neuropsychological perspective, neurosurgery is still a possibility.

March 2009 saw Grey finally leave Magnolia House. He had been allocated a small council flat, unfortunately still in Teignmouth, but the relief of not having to look over our shoulders every five minutes was almost overwhelming. The work at Magnolia now continued apace, with no interruptions. Unfortunately, all of Grey's rubbish and belongings were still scattered about the grounds in front of the south apartment, so work on the gardens was impossible.

As it was, 2009 was a very mixed year. Grey eventually had all of his belongings removed, so work was finally able to start on the gardens. Shortly after that, in the April/May of 2009, I had what I now understand to be a TIA (a transient ischaemic attack). The hospital referred to it as a 'stroke without fire'. In any event, it kept me in hospital for three days and was followed by six months of counselling. Our eldest son Tony moved in for a while to look after Ann, until I had sufficiently recovered enough to take over. The following month, a letter finally arrived from Frenchay unfortunately informing us that the decision had been taken not to proceed with the deep brain surgery. It was felt that Ann's condition had worsened and would not be helped by invasive surgery. Although there were tears, and worse from me, she seemed to accept the decision with her usual pluck, but I saw the light that usually shone so brightly in her, go out. I don't believe I have ever felt quite so useless. It seemed that when she needed me most, I couldn't deliver. With hindsight, I now believe that the TIA was partly at fault – my recovery was so slow that it hindered the positive support that Ann, I'm sure, so badly needed from me.

Unfortunately, this was quickly followed in the July with the court case against Grey, which was held at the Crown Court, Exeter on the 16th July, 2009 and, following the pattern of the previous court cases, it was held in Grey's absence. He was nevertheless found guilty and sentenced to two weeks' imprisonment and had to pay all court costs (which, of course, was never going to happen). The following day, he was arrested. Also, that same day it was confirmed that Robert was now the owner of the north apartment and the freeholder of Magnolia House.

One month later, Ann and I celebrated our 50th wedding anniversary. Once again, the boys and their wives came to the rescue and organised a memorable celebration at the local golf club. Our faces, I understand, were not a reflection of the previous six months of hell.

Looking back now, I know that there were more painful years to follow, but, for me, 2009 set a benchmark, and when I'm in that dark place, I always return to that year. 23 years had passed since her diagnosis and, like the layers of an onion, Ann had peeled back each year's layer, only to discover another one! Did she despair? I'm sure she did, but she always had a stiff upper lip.

It had all started with scratchy writing, which was almost comical by itself and held no true measure of the future. Her muscles became a little stiffer, and often a little more painful. She made a joke that she wouldn't be sewing buttons on any more – or that she wouldn't be able to sew or knit or do any kind of needlepoint. In fact, she wouldn't be able to thread a needle. As the muscles stiffen though, the whole body slows up, so everything is done in slow motion, but even when slow motion looks fast, she just carried on. Her balance became impaired and, eventually, she had no balance at all. The lack of balance brings falls, accidents and the need for walking aids. Suddenly, the word 'freezing' has a completely different meaning – and it doesn't mean being cold. No, it's what her limbs do when her body tries to move from one position to another. Ann became depressed, frustrated and angry. Where do you vent your anger while the world is being sympathetic?

Depression brings with it mood swings, a lack of sleep, a lack of appetite and a lack of self-esteem. Anxieties arise in all their depressing forms. Mood changes come, orchestrated mostly by the large and diverse amount of drugs she now had to take to combat this battalion of problems, both from without and within. 'On' and 'off' also take on a whole new meaning. If Ann's 'off' the chances are something isn't working within her cocktail of drugs – so I had to watch out for the negative thoughts. 'Off' can bring on these negative thoughts, as well as apathy, perplexity, self-loathing and self-harm. If she's 'on', she may feel well which means that the drugs are working and that's a velvet prison!

Poor Ann also had bowel and bladder problems. The rigidity of her body just creates more pain and more humiliation, and just around the corner from this is the softening of her foods because she's unable to swallow. She now gets very tired, and almost completely lacks energy, always feeling exhausted. Thank heaven for the peace of sleep! Conversation slowly disappears as she's not able to converse. Her brain needs so much extra time to assimilate and respond so that she is answering the question posed 15 minutes earlier.

In the autumn years of her Parkinson's progression, she suffered from hallucinations where her greatest fears came to taunt her and she had lengthy delusionary periods where she was just lost to this world, but has little contentment in the one she was in.

Finally, just so you get the complete package of Parkinson's Disease, dementia is likely – in my lovely girl's case it is Lewy Body Dementia – and so she is really lost to the world. In 2009, some of this was yet to happen, but oh! Oh, it's so close. I want to scream at the world about its great injustice. A more loving, kinder, sweeter person than Ann was never born. Why did someone who had so much to give and to so many people have her life shortened by all those years? And shortened in such a cruel way? I know one shouldn't ask questions of the Creator – but why? Conversely, for my part, I would have all those tough years back again, than never to have had the privilege of loving her.

Although Ann had had regular quarterly clinics at Exeter, in 2010 we threw the programme out of the window. Whether or not the refusal for deep brain surgery had been the catalyst, we'll probably never know for sure, but what was, nevertheless, quite obvious was that Ann's dyskinesia (shaking) was beginning to take over – particularly at night-time. Due to her moderate to advanced shaking, she would require a lot of hugging and caressing her body just to try and absorb some of the energy which screamed out to be released, so she could get short periods of respite. There were now times where, without the full weight of my body, literally lying to top of hers to absorb some of the energy, she would simply have thrown herself off the bed. The violent agitation in her whole body had completely taken over any rational thinking and it required all my strength to reduce the power of it.

By early 2010, her body weight was down to just under seven stone, and our routine had hardly changed for two months. One morning, I rang the hospital who informed me that there had been lengthy discussions and it had been decided to admit Ann into hospital to set up a pump which would deliver a regular fixed amount of a drug called apomorphine. It appeared that the 'duck's feet' must have been working overtime – all serenity above and frantic underneath! The initial dose would be 3mg per hour per day and it would be reinjected every 24 hours.

The first few days were purely on trial and once the trial was completed, Ann returned home. It looked as though she was carrying around her own small, personal derringer, with its own holster. The supply line for the drug was suspended below her derringer and anchored by injection into the top of her leg or stomach. She was reinjected in a different place, every 24 hours, a duty I shared with the district nurses until she went into care. Like any machine, it could go wrong and I would be informed of the error by a read-out on the machine and a high-pitched intermittent whistle. The read-out would indicate the severity of the error. We had a 24 hour emergency help line which I used frequently and at all times of the day and night during the next three months. There was still an element of fine-tuning to be done – and this had to be done in hospital – but, within two months, the hospital had achieved what they believed was an acceptable balance of drugs to cope with all the various diversifications of this incredibly complicated disease. When all looked lost, apomorphine came to the rescue.

A period of relative peace followed. Her cocktail of drugs at that time was apomorphine, sinemet-sinemet plus, clozapine, clonazepam and regular painkillers. Make no mistake – if it wasn't for teams of people like the Movement Disorder Service at Exeter, led by experienced doctors such as Vaughan Pearce, who do the research and spend hours and hours with patients like my lovely Ann, and carers like me who were allowed to ring him at any time with any concerns – I'd even rung him at his home – these little miracles wouldn't happen.

What I haven't intentionally overlooked, but will mention now, are the myriad friends coming from all walks of our life – business, theatre, golf, card groups, the Royal Air Force and last, but definitely not least, our dining group, which – bless her – I had to carry Ann out of during the last one we attended. She managed the first course and then fell asleep! That would be in early

2013. These people, and they each know who they are, will always have my heartfelt thanks. To make someone feel normal and special, even when all in front of you differs from the person you've known before, is a gift that comes straight from the Lord. It has been my honour to call them friends.

Alas, as I write this I am conscious of how many preceded Ann in their passing and the many who have since followed. One couple, although it's a little unfair to single out just one couple, I have to bring to your attention – David and Sue Last. All of our friends were special because as time went on our needs were greater than theirs, but any couple who are prepared to organise holidays to just about every destination you can think of, and then a cruise – believe me, that is loyalty. Our day-to-day problems were in their faces 24/7 – warts definitely included – and when Ann couldn't hold the cards for whist any more, which she couldn't from about 2008/9, did they give up? No! David made little stands so that she could stand the cards up – which enabled her to sort them into suits. I could go on. All of our friends did so many wonderful things, without even a thought for themselves, and that makes them very, very special people.

Almost until his death, which was in August 2011, Grey was still filing law suits against Robert and Linda Down. The last and, I believe, the final one, was regarding some Georgian door panels which Robert had received amongst an awful lot of Grey's other rubbish when he finalised the purchase of the north apartment and the freehold of Magnolia House. I can now declare that they were burnt alongside 'antique this', 'antique that' and 'antique the other'. I hope that it helps him to rest if I tell him, "I am more of an antique than any of your Georgian rubbish!"

To close this particular chapter properly, I must say I cannot carry any hatred forward. If I try and look past Grey's direct impact on Ann's health and, if I'm really generous, I must say that just as I cannot stop the Parkinson's machine from rolling on, Grey couldn't really stop his behaviour: he was a troubled soul, as much to himself as he was to others. His fault was that he took it out on those less able and who were not equipped to defend themselves. I am sure that his judgement has already taken place, so I now only feel compassion.

In a strange sort of way, with Grey now departed and all the court case stuff behind us, it meant that we could now get on with what I have always thought was the most important thing in life – looking after Ann. I never thought that she was going to get better, but I could now spend time making sure that everything she needed was available. Whether consciously or not, I tried to make the most of every day. As had been the case for some short while, I couldn't leave her unless she had a carer in, but she didn't really like carers. She either thought they were a waste of money or, in her opinion, they didn't treat her as though she were a human being. Her example of this and, I believe, one with some merit, was that, upon their arrival, they would sign-in, all smiles, check all the paperwork and make small talk with Ann until I departed. They would wave me off, make themselves a cup of tea, hardly ever asking Ann if she wanted one – probably because that would require their involvement in her care – and then they'd sit down in an armchair where they could see her and read a book. Generally, according to Ann, the routine never varied. Now I know that this sounds cynical, but the truth is that very few private carers do anything more than is absolutely necessary in order to keep the client safe. Their argument is that's what they are there for. For me, the issue was not debateable – so I got rid of the carers.

The danger of that is, of course, that I was then relying on family and friends to fill in the inevitable times when I just had to go out, and that can put a strain on relationships. Nevertheless, it was no great hardship not to do some of the regular things I liked to do, like golf, keep fit and so on. So, unless it was essential, like on a Thursday morning, because I still had a small part-time job doing accounting work for friends which I had done for the best part of the last 20 years, either friends would look after Ann or, if need be, I'd take her with me. But, other than that, I made sure that everything else we could do together.

CHAPTER 19

A HEART OF PAIN

This is not a medical journal. It is not going to tell you what or what not to do under a certain set of circumstances. In fact, it's not going to tell you anything other than what it is like to live with someone who had Parkinson's Disease for nearly 30 years. It hasn't always been easy, but it was always worthwhile. Parkinson's Disease is so different in so many different ways in just about every sufferer. I know that because I've spent time with other sufferers. I have sat for endless hours in clinics, surgeries, hospitals and myriad well-meaning organisations that are set up to help those with Parkinson's and, to date, several hundred books have been written about it. Yet if I learned anything, it is that, as your loved one's Parkinson's develops, you develop. As the stages of Parkinson's change, you change. As they become more wilful, you become more helpful. When they're weak, you have to be strong. When they get frustrated anxious, depressed or tired, you have to be there even more, love them even more. Never let them believe that they are not worthwhile.

It's true to say that by the time I arrived at the 26th year of caring, I felt that I was pretty knowledgeable about the disease. But nothing – *nothing* – could have prepared me for the years ahead, because nothing that had gone before was going to be of any help in what I was about to experience.

Up until the beginning of 2012, Ann had experienced some quite severe delusions and hallucinations and medical science had drugs standing by to combat the rats in the bed, the red spiders crawling up the wall, furry creatures just around the corner, the other people in the room and the three-way conversations with them. There was also the endless need for her to clean out her drawers, sort out all the clothing, dispose of all the items she felt were not needed and wash out the cupboards. During 2012, over and above all that I've mentioned, there was something else though, a something else that felt almost personal – a furtive look, severe mood changes, unusual behaviour changes. A passing comment, "I know, you know," with a knowledgeable tap to the side of the nose. This went on for some months in various forms, quite often very late into the night and occasionally through the night. Our relationship seemed to change. Now I was the centre of her fear.

I finally called the crisis team, after a particularly taxing night and asked to have her admitted to the hospital, where subsequently she was diagnosed with Parkinson's Disease Dementia (Lewy Body). From 2012 to 2014, she showed continual signs of the development of the dementia. There is no doubt in my mind that the absolute worst aspect of the period mentioned – and probably of the time right up until she finally went into care – was that I always seemed to be at the heart of her worst fears or her nightmares. It would take me hours to even coax her to come into bed because she believed that I had engaged a third person to harm her if she moved. The battles were usually only won because she became too tired to compete. She would eventually fall asleep and I would carry her to bed.

I know about the medical reasoning for the above behaviours, but living with it is quite another matter. My heart was always in pain. It might be useful at this stage just to give a bit of background about the symptoms of Lewy Body and the effect it had on Ann during that two to two and a half year period of her life.

It is not only difficult for the medical services to diagnose LBD (Lewy Body Dementia), it is sometimes impossible to diagnose when it occurs. So many of the early problems of hallucinations, delusions, anxiety and paranoia are also some of the later symptoms of Parkinson's, so there is, I've found, an awful lot of cross-overs between the two conditions, particularly when the final diagnosis is Parkinson's Disease Dementia. The two names only come together when the dementia starts. It is difficult to differentiate one from the other. This is often made worse because the early symptoms of LBD are not dissimilar from Alzheimer's too. In Ann's case, the symptoms appeared much later as she'd then had Parkinson's Disease for about 26 years (although it is now my belief that all the signs were there much earlier).

The difficulty I found – and which delayed the final diagnosis – was that, for about three years, many of the symptoms of LBD were an extension or exaggeration of what had gone before. Although I wasn't aware at the time, I have since found out that once a long-term Parkinson's sufferer contracts Parkinson's Disease Dementia, their average lifespan is five to seven years from that point.

During 2012 to 2014, there had been a general escalation of all the symptoms described earlier and, in the main, they were mostly manageable. It was during 2014 where I seemed to become more and more of the problem and much more the enemy in Ann's eyes.

Back in February 2012, there was a period of enforced respite. My third and final hernia had been nagging away for some time and it had now reached a point where I had to be operated upon. I had explained all the details to Ann and she agreed to go into the Glendale Nursing Home, the home nearest to us and one we had used before. Unfortunately, the time required for me to convalesce from the operation stretched into five weeks. Overlooking all of the difficulties of mobile phones and the fact that she'd lost hers within 10 days, I was still able to communicate with her regularly and friends and family visited as often as they could. It, nevertheless highlighted in so many ways, that Glendale were now ill-equipped to cope with Ann's increasing problems. Her return home was difficult from a care viewpoint too, as I wasn't really as strong as I needed to be. But, you know what, I would have had her back under any circumstances. She was, after all, my lovely girl.

During the next couple of years, up to the end of 2014, they did have to increase certain drugs just to contain some of her more frequent violent outbursts. We did manage, nevertheless, to secure a holiday through RAFA (The Royal Air Force Association) in September of 2013. We were so grateful for this opportunity as the hotel was really an upmarket nursing home. They gave us a large room on the maximum care floor which for me, was wonderful. And, although I never left her, other than for the odd short walk, someone was constantly there, 24 hrs a day and seven days a week. When she fell asleep at night, which was usually at about 19.00 to 20.00 hrs, the duty floor nurse would always poke her head around the door and ask if she could get me a whisky from the bar. As I write this, I find it very difficult not to break down when I think of all the kindnesses people showed, even though they didn't know us very well. Nothing was too much trouble. The nights were sometimes difficult for Ann, but help was always at hand. But the days were warm and pleasant with lots of walks, although often she would fall asleep in her wheelchair. Too soon though, it was over and I almost wept the day we had to leave. Such kindness is so difficult to find, combined with tolerance and nursing expertise – but we both felt a little refreshed after our break.

The problems continued into and through 2014 and Ann was hospitalised on three occasions. The first two occasions were as a result of falls which resulted in cracked ribs, a broken thumb and dislocated fingers. The third time, which was at the end of October 2014 was, for me at least, considerably more painful. The problems started in the early afternoon when she refused to take her tablets because she felt she was being poisoned. She became a little hysterical and said that she wanted to speak to David. I told her that I was David, but she just stared at me and asked me if I thought she was stupid – she knew what David looked like! I was just there to harm her. She eventually backed off into the kitchen, her eyes never leaving mine, just flicking about like a frightened cornered animal. She said she wanted me to leave so she could think. This I did. I sat on the bed and wept, knowing that if she left the kitchen I would at least see her and make sure she was alright.

After a short while, I returned and she still looked furtive and frightened. She told me that she knew that somebody was in the bathroom waiting for her to pass so that he or she could attack her. I eventually agreed to open all the doors of the rooms adjacent to or between the kitchen and the sitting room so that she could see that there was nobody there. After an awful lot of coaxing and coercing, I eventually managed to get her into the sitting room where she would do less harm to herself if she fell. She wouldn't let me near her, but she said that I could sit down on the floor some distance from where she was sitting. I just kept talking to her, telling her who I was and that I didn't mean her any harm. She was not convinced, but tiredness started to take over and she became very quiet. I asked her if she would like a pillow to rest her head on. She agreed, but I had to throw it to her and not approach her.

When I thought that she had fallen asleep, I rang the crisis team who came and took her off to hospital – it was 31st October 2014. Upon her arrival, they sedated her and she was still asleep when I left in the early hours of the following day. That night, I wept until my body ached and I fell asleep on top of the bed, fully clothed. If I'm honest, I think they were tears of self-pity – or tears for what might have been. I almost look back on this period in a daze.

At the time, the only positive thing for me was that her illness had clearly reached a point where my input was useless – I just wasn't helping. So although the team were unhappy to see her back in hospital, I think that they also realised that it needed a conscientious effort on their part to sort out her drugs, once and for all, so that I was able to manage her better when she returned home.

During the six or seven weeks she was in hospital, her behaviour, based only on my daily visits, was never the same. Certainly, that was the case during the first three or four weeks. Some days, she seemed to be hyperactive and apparently difficult to control, often refusing to leave the toilet or wandering off to explore, which usually ended in falls. There wasn't a day that passed, apparently, that she didn't resist taking her medication. Usually, she told me, it was because they were trying to poison her. And yet, on other days – and this would be for days at a time – she would be completely docile, usually more asleep than awake. They were also having difficulty in getting her to eat, so she continued to lose weight.

Over those weeks, I questioned every staff member I could find regarding these fluctuations in her behaviour. I eventually found out, through one of the consultants, that they were re-trialling the balance of her drugs, regarding both the Parkinson's requirements and Lewy Body's requirements – which, in essence, meant that they were increasing her anti-psychotic tablets to create a balance that was both right for her and clearly manageable for them. A more docile Ann!

As the weeks progressed, that is exactly what happened. By week five, Ann became quieter, more docile and usually quite tearful. She regularly expressed a desire to know where she was, assuming, I believe, that I'd had her put away! She slowly began to accept her surroundings and felt that she was 'in charge' of the ward, questioning all visitors upon their arrival and advising them accordingly. She even asked me to consider purchasing the ward next door, so that I was always near.

Leaving was always difficult, but I am certain that she came to believe that I would return the following day – which I always did. Early the following week, I was told that a meeting had been set up on the following Friday morning to discuss Ann's future. The meeting comprised of consultants, nurses, a matron, psychologists and social services with myself and another relative also in attendance.

It probably highlights how naïve I was because I thought that this was a meeting regarding the additional help at home that I would need now that the drug issue had been resolved. My eldest son Tony, came with me and I believe that he knew what to expect, even if I didn't. They didn't come straight out and say it but each one in turn spoke about the problems they'd found, the surmised problems to come and, as a result, how Ann should be placed in full-time nursing care.

Well, I just broke down, but I still tried to express that I felt I could look after this calmer, more docile Ann and that she didn't now need to go into a nursing home. The discussion continued without me, with Tony speaking for me because all I could do was cry. I was absolutely distraught. I could not believe that everything we had been through had led us to this.

Over and above my weeping and the noise of the general discussion, I heard a voice say, "But surely you must have seen this coming, Mr. Dean?"

I had no answer. I just walked out, mumbling that I would return in a short while.

When I returned, slightly calmer, the numbers in the room had reduced to three – there was only Tony, the matron and the social services lady left. The rest had moved on to other important issues, leaving behind the crater from their bombshell.

There was never a heartfelt acceptance of this decision but, after time and much discussion, I reached a heart-wrenching conclusion. Could I really give Ann the care she so badly needed? Was I physically capable of continuing to attend her every need? How long would it be before I was also in a care home?

Almost in a daze, but with the strength of my sons and the guidance of the social services lady, we finally secured a nursing home for Ann in Dawlish, called Palm Court. Over the next couple of weeks, every day I tried to explain to Ann why I couldn't take her home and why she needed the special care of a professional nursing home. These discussions usually fell on deaf ears and were met by a blank face – a face that usually just stared back at me and rarely asked questions. It was almost as though she had given up. But she did still feel something because I could see the signs of distress etched into her face. My heart was broken.

On the 18th December 2014, I was at the care home awaiting Ann's arrival. As a result of the report that the home had received from all the various hospital agencies, it was assumed that Ann could be troublesome and that she should, therefore, be confined to a severe dementia floor with controlled access. This was the very worst thing that could have happened to Ann and it took me three weeks of pleading her case and imploring the management at Palm Court to reconsider her placement in light of the Ann they had come to know in that short time, so they would give her a room on a floor with like-minded residents and not those close to sectioning. Bless them, they agreed and, in early January, they moved her to a lovely room overlooking the activities area, with free access to the dining room, sitting room and all the corridors in between.

There were daily activities in the sitting room, such as art classes, music classes and games, many of which Ann attended. I had her room redecorated in her favourite colour with new curtains and brought our own furniture from home. I even had the piece of ground outside her window landscaped into an ornamental garden, full of her favourite plants. If this sounds as though I was also filling a need of my own, you would be right. What I did was wholly for Ann, but it did help to lessen the guilt in me that never went away.

Ann slowly settled in. We went from fewer tearful days sometimes to short periods where there were no tears at all. It wasn't long before she was 'in charge' of her floor and needed to know all the comings and goings of visitors. She would frequently talk about her favourite nurses or carers and she very rarely complained about the food. In fact, the chef would come up to her room daily and ask her what she would like to eat – partly because there were some foods which she couldn't swallow, but mainly because they were just very nice people and really cared.

Whenever the possibility arose, we always went out. If it was slightly inclement, I would take her for a drive and stop for tea somewhere. She particularly liked Powderham Castle. If it was warm, I would wrap her up and we would walk – or in Ann's case, wheel – around Dawlish, usually taking in the bowls if they were playing. We would also occasionally meet up with friends, usually David and Sue Last, and have tea or her very favourite, a large bowl of chips with lots of tomato sauce. The various cafés got to know us quite well.

I can honestly say that, almost daily, whether we had to stay in the home or we were able to get out, my love for this lady just grew and grew to a point sometimes that I thought my heart would burst. Just to see her gave me the most enormous joy. And, although sometimes she thought I was someone else, usually one of the boys, the sheer pleasure on her face when I walked into her room made my heart ache with love – and what did it really matter that she was in a care home? We frequently relived our 50-plus years of marriage and all the houses, counties and countries where we had lived – we still knew that joy of love.

In about the late spring of that year, I had put together two large montages of photographs, one to place in Ann's room and one for myself. The one in Ann's room was every possible photo taken of all the people that attended our 50th wedding anniversary, which was, with few exceptions, everybody we had befriended over all those years. She loved it and spent hours just examining the photos. I know that it helped her relive the memories of our relationships with each of them over the decades. The other montage was completely self-indulgent. I had collated 30 or 40 photographs of my lovely girl from when we first met in 1958 until just before she entered the care home: Ann's life, with me, as seen through the camera for every decade, and in almost all situations – all in one frame. I love it! Not a day passes that I don't want to spend time staring at it, steeped in the memories those photographs convey. There, she is, alive for me in every year of every decade of our married life.

There were some trying times too, mostly for the staff in the care home, because of Ann's fluctuating behaviour as the Lewy Body disease took hold, coupled with the need to decrease and/or increase her drugs to keep her calm and improve her quality of life. By June however, she seemed to be quite well and most of the time she was very quiet and quite dreamy. I believe that, once again, they had increased her anti-psychotic drugs.

That all changed rather dramatically on the 18th July though, when she accidentally slipped off her bed and the neck of her nightie caught on the bedside table's adjustment knob, effectively garrotting her. If it had not been for the timely intervention of a carer, she would certainly have died.

As it was, when I received the call from the home at about 19.30 hrs, the emergency services were already there and, upon my arrival, informed me that they didn't think she would survive. She was propped up in her bed, blue in colour with no real signs of life. I just broke down. The paramedics said that they would take her to hospital, but that I should prepare myself.

One of the boys – Colin, if I remember correctly – met me at Accident & Emergency. The colour had returned to Ann's face in that it wasn't blue anymore, but she still hadn't regained consciousness. In the early hours, still unconscious, they transferred her to a ward. We left at their suggestion at about 03.00 hrs. They were still trying to resuscitate her. After a sleepless few hours, I rang at about 09.00 hrs and was informed that she had just woken up and indicated that she needed a drink. Who said that there isn't a God!

She stayed in hospital for about a week. In that time, she regained some of her former health, but was unable to speak and was on a liquid only diet. By the beginning of August, she was back in the care home. The accident – and that is what it was, just a freak thing – had been investigated accordingly. The incident had clearly weakened her though. She had lost weight, was now on soft foods only and seemed very introspective and still had great difficulty in speaking. I have always believed, in hindsight, that the accident was the beginning of the end. At the time though, I was just overjoyed that she had survived and was back in the care of Palm Court.

CHAPTER 20

THE BEGINNING OF THE END

Over the next few months, it was just a series of ups and downs. During September, she had a really bad urine infection, followed by an equally bad chest infection. Her weight continued to drop, obviously because she was unable to take sufficient nourishment, but the staff at the care home were absolutely brilliant. They provided pillows between or against all exposed joints, so that they didn't rub and they always turned her very carefully, ensuring that she was facing the door, as opposed to the wall, when they knew that I would be arriving. By October, the chest infection had taken its toll and she was very frail. My heart would frequently break when I saw her, but she always managed a smile of recognition when I entered her room.

During October, it was agreed to stop some of her drugs because she was almost totally immobile and they just seemed to be working against her and were doing more harm than good. However, by the end of October, it became quite obvious that the dyskinesia had returned with a vengeance, so they had to restart the apomorphine pump. This made her a little more comfortable.

Although November saw her becoming increasingly frail and unable to move, there were many treasured moments. Because the staff always turned her to face the door, her eyes would become a little brighter when I arrived. Up until she passed away, I always laid my head on her pillow facing her with our eyes just inches apart and told her how much I loved her. Although she was unable to move her face, her eyes told me that she understood. Although I weep with this memory, as I'm doing now, it's a memory that I never want to lose. It's a memory that encapsulates the love we had for each other, regardless of the difficulties that life threw at us.

By the middle of December, she had survived two prognoses that she would pass away during those respective weekends – only to be there on the Monday! This was one lady who wasn't going to conform – she would go when she was ready. And she did. At 09.34 on the 19th December 2015.

When I arrived at 10.05, she was in exactly the same position as I had left her the previous day. Her eyes were still open but now they were sightless. I laid my head on her pillow, weeping unashamedly. I stared at my beautiful girl – a beauty now that only I could see. She was still my beloved Ann.

Printed in Great Britain
by Amazon